3
Popcorn
Nuts
Candy
Granola Bars
Cereal

The Diversion

**Even the book morphs!
Flip the pages
and check it out!**

Look for other ANIMORPHS® titles by K.A. Applegate:

#1 *The Invasion*
#2 *The Visitor*
#3 *The Encounter*
#4 *The Message*
#5 *The Predator*
#6 *The Capture*
#7 *The Stranger*
#8 *The Alien*
#9 *The Secret*
#10 *The Android*
#11 *The Forgotten*
#12 *The Reaction*
#13 *The Change*
#14 *The Unknown*
#15 *The Escape*
#16 *The Warning*
#17 *The Underground*
#18 *The Decision*
#19 *The Departure*
#20 *The Discovery*
#21 *The Threat*
#22 *The Solution*
#23 *The Pretender*
#24 *The Suspicion*
#25 *The Extreme*
#26 *The Attack*
#27 *The Exposed*
#28 *The Experiment*
#29 *The Sickness*
#30 *The Reunion*
#31 *The Conspiracy*
#32 *The Separation*
#33 *The Illusion*
#34 *The Prophecy*
#35 *The Proposal*
#36 *The Mutation*
#37 *The Weakness*
#38 *The Arrival*
#39 *The Hidden*
#40 *The Other*
#41 *The Familiar*
#42 *The Journey*
#43 *The Test*
#44 *The Unexpected*
#45 *The Revelation*
#46 *The Deception*
#47 *The Resistance*
#48 *The Return*

<MEGAMORPHS>

#1 *The Andalite's Gift*
#2 *In the Time of Dinosaurs*
#3 *Elfangor's Secret*
#4 *Back to Before*

the andalite chronicles

The Hork-Bajir Chronicles
Visser
The Ellimist Chronicles

ALTERNAMORPHS

The First Journey
The Next Passage

ANIMORPHS®

The Diversion

K.A. Applegate

AN
APPLE
PAPERBACK

SCHOLASTIC INC.
New York Toronto London Auckland Sydney
Mexico City New Delhi Hong Kong

The author wishes to thank Lisa Harkrader for her help in preparing this manuscript.

For Larry, Ashley, and Austin

And for Michael and Jake

Cover illustration by David B. Mattingly
Art Direction/Design by Karen Hudson/Ursula Albano

ISBN 0-439-11523-X

12 11 10 9 8 7 6 5 4 3 2 1 2 3 4 5 6/0

Printed in the U.S.A.
First Scholastic printing, January 2001

CHAPTER 1

My name is Tobias. And I was one hungry bird.

I was perched in a tree at the edge of my meadow. A meadow grown crisp and brown from too many days without rain. The sun blazed overhead. Wind whispered through the weeds.

And among the rippling stalks, one, then two twisted slightly in another direction. I dug my talons into the bark of the branch and waited.

Listened.

Mouse feet scrabbled against hard-packed dirt. Mouse teeth chewed through the shell of a seed. Chewed. Stopped. Scrabbled.

Stopped.

I waited.

Nothing. No sound. No movement. The mouse remained still. Also listening? Waiting?

I tensed. Cocked my head.

And thought, not for the first time, about the irony of my hunt. In my old life, my life as a boy, I was the mouse. The prey. Stalked by predators bent on flushing my head down the men's room toilet. Scurrying to find a hiding place. Rarely succeeding.

Another irony: In my old life, my life as prey, food was not a problem. I was on the free lunch program at school. So I knew exactly where my next meal was coming from. Overheated ladies in hair nets slapped it on a tray and handed it to me.

Movement. Small. A single blade of grass tipped toward a bare patch of dirt. Claws scritched against earth.

The mouse was coming out into the open.

I opened my wings, pushed off the branch, and circled, high above the meadow, then began to descend. My shadow grew larger and darker over the patch of dirt.

Weeds twitched, first one, then the next, as the mouse moved closer to open ground.

Dust billowed out from the undergrowth. Then a nose. Brown. Whiskered. I raked my talons forward.

The mouse scuttled out, completely unprotected now. I dropped. In a split second the mouse would be mine. In a split second my hunger would be —

No!

Scales. A flash of yellow. Fangs sinking into the mouse's flesh.

That's when I heard it. An ominous rattle.

Yeah. Like I needed a warning. I flapped hard and rose, talons empty. I was hungry but I wasn't stupid. I wouldn't fight a six-foot rattlesnake over a poisoned mouse.

I climbed higher, glided above the meadow, and watched the snake devour my lunch. A diamondback that had lain coiled, waiting, motionless, in the very spot I'd been watching. In the meadow. My meadow.

I circled and swooped back to my branch.

Would a normal hawk have seen it? Maybe. Probably.

Your normal red-tailed hawk, equipped with the standard-issue hawk brain, has a basic train of thought. Hunger. Food. Kill. Eat. Brilliant in its simplicity. The hawk is not distracted by ironic musings. The hawk doesn't reminisce about toilets and school cafeterias.

But I'm not a normal hawk. I'm not a normal anything. I'm a kid trapped in a bird's body. Like nothing else on this or any other planet. A species of one.

I used to be human. Fully human, or at least

that's what I thought. Until my friends and I met a dying alien warrior, an Andalite prince named Elfangor.

Elfangor-Sirinial-Shamtul. Strange how, even then, before I knew who he was, before I knew about my own past, I was drawn to him. Connected in a way the other Animorphs hadn't been.

That's what we are, my friends and I. Animorphs. Animal morphers. We can acquire the DNA of another animal, then become that animal. Elfangor gave us that power. He gave it to us as a weapon, the only weapon we have in our battle to save Earth from evil, parasitic aliens.

Yeerks. Slimy. Gray. Not much bigger than the field mouse I'd been stalking, but completely lacking the mouse's senses. Yeerks are deaf, blind. They have no feet or hands. If you saw a Yeerk in its natural state, you'd think it was an overgrown slug. And you probably wouldn't be any more afraid of it than of a slug.

But you should be.

A Yeerk slithers in through your ear canal and flattens itself out over the surface of your brain. It wriggles into all the crevices and valleys. Taps into every brain circuit and nerve ending. Taps into your very existence.

You become a Controller, and it's an ironic name because you have absolutely *no* control.

You can't speak, move, eat, even go to the bathroom unless the Yeerk wants you to. You watch as the Yeerk spreads evil and hatred using your hands, your voice. You can't scream. You can't run away.

The Yeerks enslaved entire sentient species on other planets. The Gedds. The Taxxons. The Hork-Bajir. Now they've come to Earth, to enslave humans.

And we, the Animorphs, are fighting them alone. A few things help level the playing field. Kandrona, for one. If a Yeerk doesn't feed on Kandrona rays every three days, it dies.

We also get help from the Chee, an android race hardwired against violence. They can't fight, but they've infiltrated the Yeerk organization and feed us information when they can.

And, of course, morphing. An Andalite technology. Though it seems unbelievable, the Yeerks still think we're Andalites.

Morphing is a powerful weapon, but it has rules. 1) You can't change directly from one morph to another without first returning to your natural body. 2) You have to acquire DNA directly from an animal. You can't acquire it from another morph. 3) You can't stay in morph for more than two hours at a time, because if you do, you stay permanently. You become what the Andalites call a *nothlit*.

Like me.

I stayed in hawk morph too long, and now I'm not a human in hawk morph.

I'm a hawk.

I was able to regain my morphing ability and through a little fancy time-bending by a powerful being called the Ellimist, I gained another morph. My old self. My human self. For two hours at a time I can morph Tobias the kid. Be human, at least physically. Then I must return to hawk or I'll lose my morphing capability altogether. I'll be out of the fight.

So, while I watched the snake digest my mouse, I spotted an eagle soaring toward me. A bald eagle, carrying lunch in its talons. Not a mouse or a rabbit. A paper bag. Even from this distance I could see the golden arches.

Rachel was bringing McDonald's. Rachel, my own personal cafeteria-lady-in-a-hair-net.

Don't ever tell her I said that.

CHAPTER 2

Rachel drifted over the meadow, her profile stark against the sun. She spiraled down and dropped the McDonald's bag in the grass under my tree.

<You do know there's a rattlesnake in your meadow, don't you?> She landed and began to demorph.

<Uh, yeah.> I flapped down from my perch. <We met briefly.>

Rachel's feathers melted together, swirled into tan Rachel skin. Her wings stretched into arms. Legs shifted forward with a sickening crack.

That's one thing I'll never get used to — the sounds. Body parts twisting, tearing, being ab-

sorbed and re-formed. It doesn't hurt. It should, but it doesn't. The Andalites worked some kind of painkiller into the technology.

But they didn't manage to kill the sound.

Rachel's body shot up to human size. A human with bird-of-prey eyes. I've never been sure if Rachel's human eyes are more intense because of the eagle, or if the eagle's eyes are so intense because they're Rachel's. They were clear blue now instead of amber, but they still held a deadly gaze.

She fixed that gaze on me now. "Look, before you get your feathers in a wad, just listen. I know I don't have to baby you. I know you can take care of yourself. But I also know your happy little meadow is about to dry up, and the weather guy on Channel 6 isn't predicting rain any time soon." She pulled a Big Mac from the bag. "So eat this and don't give me grief, okay?"

That's one of the things I like best about Rachel. I don't need to admit to her that hawk life can be a little stressful. She just knows. And tries to help. But she doesn't feel sorry for me. Or at least, she doesn't let me see her feel sorry for me. She lets me have my dignity.

Too bad you can't eat dignity. I watched her open the Big Mac box and set it on the grass.

"I know you have to eat yours as a hawk." She pulled out another Big Mac and two large fries.

"But at least we can hang out for a while. A little while."

Uh-huh. I wasn't paying much attention to the conversation. My hawk brain focused on the usual. Hunger. Food. Kill. Okay, maybe we could skip "kill" just this once. Eat.

But my human brain remembered something more: The pure pleasure of sinking my teeth into three inches of hamburger and bun. The crunch of lettuce and onion. The grease and cheese and special sauce combining as I chewed. And the fries. Was there ever a more perfect food than a McDonald's french fry? Fresh from the fryer, while they're still steaming. Crisp and salty and so soft in the middle they —

"Tobias?" Rachel was staring at me, frowning. "I asked if you want me to take the pickles off."

<Um, no.> *Get a grip, Tobias. You're turning into Ax.* <Just pull off one of the hamburger patties. I'll eat it first, then morph human and eat the rest with you.>

She peeled the Big Mac apart and set one of the patties in the grass. I ripped off a chunk of meat and wrangled it sideways into my beak.

"You know, Tobias," she said, "we have very weird dates."

I devoured the hamburger, then stood completely still for a moment, savoring the full feel-

ing in my stomach. My hawk belly was happy. My hawk body would survive another day.

Time to feed the human. I focused on Tobias the kid.

SPRRROOOOOOT!

I shot up to my full human height. The sudden shift knocked me off balance, and I teetered on twelve-inch talons. Morphing isn't predictable. As I lifted my wings for support, my feathers melted and evaporated, leaving only pale pink nubs on my skin.

I looked down. I was a nearly naked bird the size of a human kid. A giant plucked chicken in spandex.

"Attractive," said Rachel.

Hollow bird bones thickened and — *snap* — realigned. Internal organs shifted and stretched. My shoulders widened, neck grew long. Arms and fingers emerged from stubby wings. The scales on my legs disappeared and human flesh emerged. Talons split into toes. My beak melted and formed a nose and lips. Round bird eyes slid forward and became ovals.

I touched my arm. The pink chicken bumps dissolved into smooth beige skin. Pale still, but smooth.

I was human.

Rachel smiled. "Much better."

"Thanks," I said. Or at least, that's what I meant to say. What came out was, "Grrrx." I hadn't used my human voice in a while. I cleared my throat, limbered my jaw, and tried again. "Thank you."

We sat side by side in the grass with our backs against the tree. I bit into my Big Mac. And sighed. Well, actually I moaned. Out loud. Grease and cheese and special sauce dribbled down my chin.

Rachel shook her head and handed me a napkin.

Which would've been embarrassing if I hadn't been so involved with my lunch. Sometimes I forget normal human things. Like my old locker combination or which months have thirty-one days or how to work the token machine at the arcade. Useless information to a hawk, of course. Still, it scared me a little. Like I'd crossed a line and might not ever get back. Or worse, I'd forget so many things that given the opportunity, I might not want to get back.

But I hadn't forgotten the Big Mac. Or the fries. As long as I had fast food, I had hope.

Rachel brushed an ant off her leg. "You need to get a picnic table," she said. "Or at least a couple of lawn chairs."

"Oh, yeah, Rachel, definitely low profile. A

hawk with patio furniture. Maybe I could get a barbecue grill, too, and some bamboo torch lights."

"Very funny." She crumpled her empty burger box and stuffed it into the bag. "Shut up and eat so we can get out of here. Cassie's called a meeting, and Jake says we all have to be there."

"Ah." I swallowed a fry. "The X-Men have nothing on us, do they?"

"Got that right."

CHAPTER 3

"Let me get this straight." Marco shredded a piece of hay. "They wanted blood samples. Not cash. Not drugs. Blood."

We were in Cassie's barn. The Wildlife Rehabilitation Clinic. Sort of a homeless shelter for wounded animals. Cassie's parents are both veterinarians. Her mom works at The Gardens, a combination zoo/amusement park where we've acquired most of our battle morphs. Her dad runs the clinic here on their farm. Cassie helps him out.

At the moment she was inside a big wire pen, doctoring a doe that had been shot in the thigh. The rest of us were trying not to focus on the hypodermic needle in her hand.

"The rest of us" could've starred in one of those weepy movies on Lifetime. Jake: Rachel's cousin, Cassie's true love, and the leader of our little band of misfits. Ax the alien: Elfangor's little brother and, strange as it sounds, my uncle. Marco: Jake's best friend and Ax's part-time roommate. Rachel, of course: Cassie's best friend, the girl dating out of her species. And me: Tobias. Bird-boy. On lookout duty in the rafters.

Cassie stroked the deer's neck. "It's okay, girl." She closed the pen and turned to face us. "All I know is what my mom said. Two men broke into her veterinary ward last night. It wasn't the usual smash and grab, and no, they weren't after drugs, which surprised Mom, too. They wanted blood samples, specific blood samples. Tiger. Elephant. Eagle. Rhino and grizzly. Gorilla and wolf."

Rachel stared at her. "Our battle morphs."

"Right." Cassie nodded. "They showed no interest in the warthogs or baboons. One of Mom's lab techs stumbled in on them. They really roughed him up, especially —" She glanced at me. "Especially when he told them The Gardens didn't have a red-tailed hawk."

Seven pairs of eyes, including Ax's stalk eyes, gazed up at the rafters. I turned away to preen a wing.

Cassie went on. "The lab tech said they'd been cold and methodical up to that point, but when they couldn't get the hawk sample, they just went nuts. Like they were afraid to leave without it."

"Yeah, I bet," said Marco. "I bet they were peeing their pants wondering how to explain the concept of failure to Visser One."

Visser One. Evil incarnate. The Yeerk in charge of the invasion of Earth, recently promoted from Visser Three.

Rachel nodded. "Our battle morphs? The Gardens? Nutso thieves on a mission for hawk blood? Definitely Yeerks."

"Uh, yeah," Jake agreed. "But the Chee haven't heard anything, not even rumors. And we haven't intercepted Yeerk communications about a new project. Whatever they're up to, it's at the highest level. We don't want to do anything stupid. We need to really think this through."

"Okay, so we'll think it through and then we'll do something stupid," said Marco. "First question: Why do the Yeerks need animal blood? Have they invented a new way to morph?"

<Invented?> Ax's stalk eyes narrowed to slits. <Yeerks do not invent. They steal. Everything they have, they have taken from other species. Most notably the Andalites. They do not have the

intelligence — or the integrity — to invent a morphing technique of their own.>

Did I mention Andalites can be a wee bit arrogant?

Cassie looked at Jake.

"I think Ax is right," he said. "They're after something bigger. Tom brought home a flyer yesterday. The Sharing is sponsoring a huge blood drive."

Tom was Jake's older brother.

Tom was a Controller, a high-ranking member of The Sharing. The front organization for the Yeerks.

Cassie took a deep breath. "Here's what I think. There's only one reason the Yeerks would suddenly be interested in blood. DNA. They're collecting samples of our morph animals, and they're collecting as many human samples as they can." She looked at us. "They're searching for humans with strands of animal DNA in their blood."

Silence.

"Which means —" Marco sighed.

"They know we're human," said Rachel.

CHAPTER 4

They. As in Visser One.

The only Yeerk ever to infest an Andalite. Until now he'd been convinced we Animorphs were Andalites, too.

Which was somewhat surprising because the former Visser One had discovered we were human. By keeping our secret, she hoped to destroy her adversary. The Andalite-Controller, then Visser Three.

But we destroyed her.

The former Visser One was a human-Controller. And her host was Marco's mom.

Very long story short. We raided the Yeerk pool and rescued Marco's mom. The human. The Yeerk in her head tried to escape, but was killed.

And our secret died with it.

Or so we'd thought.

"The Yeerks are probably collecting human blood from as many different sources as they can," said Jake. "Hospitals, doctors' offices, labs. Now this blood drive. So." He looked at us. "Has anybody given blood since we started acquiring morphs?"

Rachel shook her head.

"I've been afraid to," said Cassie. "Who knows what's floating around in my veins."

"I've been too busy saving the planet." Marco.

"The planet is grateful." Jake rolled his eyes. "But it's not you we need to worry about, Marco. The Yeerks think you and your family are dead, so even if they had a sample of your blood containing animal DNA, it wouldn't lead them anywhere. Ax is an Andalite, so that's not a problem. And Tobias . . ."

<Tobias hasn't given blood since he magically turned into a bird,> I said.

"Right." Jake smiled at me — a grim smile edged with guilt — and nodded. "Which narrows it down to Cassie, Rachel, and me." He turned to Cassie and Rachel. "Think hard. Any doctor visits? Trips to the school nurse?"

Cassie shook her head. Rachel shrugged.

"Are you sure? What about when we all came down with the Andalite flu? The *yamphut*."

"Oh, man." Rachel shut her eyes. "My mom did haul me to the doctor. I don't think they took blood, but I had a really high fever. Part of that time is just blanked out. But that was a while ago. If they took blood, it's long gone by now." She looked at Cassie. "Isn't it?"

"I don't know," Cassie admitted. "I don't know how long labs keep blood samples. Or data on blood samples."

"So." Rachel, eyes wide. "It could still be in a freezer somewhere. With my name on it."

<Don't even think that,> I said. <It's such a long shot.>

"Yeah." Rachel shook her head. "But we can't take that chance. If the Yeerks find me, they find us all. They'll slide a Yeerk into my head and then we're dead or worse, infested, and so are our families." She looked up at me. "And everyone we care about."

<And the free Hork-Bajir,> said Ax. <They have been forced to relocate once, in spite of our assistance. Without our help they easily could be captured, their colony destroyed.>

"Maybe," said Cassie. "Look, the Yeerks don't know we're human. Yet. They only suspect. If we really were Andalites, we'd want them to

waste time and manpower analyzing human blood samples, right? So if we bust in, destroy their project, we only prove we're not Andalites."

"Better than the alternative," Rachel argued. "We can stop the Yeerks, and yeah, they'll know we're human, but they won't know which humans. Or we can let them continue till they find us. Which they will."

"There's another option," said Jake. "We can get inside, find out what they know. Then decide what to do. The research is probably on a computer somewhere, at whatever company the Yeerks are using as a front. If we can get our hands on it, maybe we can destroy any incriminating data without the Yeerks catching on. They continue their research and come up blank. Ax, is that something you can handle?"

<Of course, Prince Jake.> Ax whipped his tail forward. <We need only find the correct facility.>

"Not a problem," said Marco. "We hack into the computer system of every blood bank, hospital, and clinic on the planet. The one we can't get into, the one with the extraterrestrial firewall, that'll be the Yeerks."

CHAPTER 5

I figured Ax and Marco would find the blood bank, Jake would call another meeting, we'd infiltrate the place and destroy any incriminating information.

Good guys win and go home.

I flew from the hayloft. The meeting was over. The sun was setting, the air beginning to cool.

Below me, Marco and Ax slipped into the little strip of woods that led from the barn to Ax's scoop. I knew they'd soon be logging on to their souped-up Mac, hacking into blood bank computers. They'd find me when they needed me, when it was time to plan the mission. In the meantime, I had other things to worry about.

Like how to eat without being eaten.

Not that I'd ever actually starve. Rachel would see to that. But what self-respecting hawk lets his girlfriend feed him? Lets her buy vitamin drops for him at Petsmart? Lets her fix a spot in her sock drawer so he has a cozy spot to sleep on dark and stormy nights? A hawk shouldn't wake up smelling like dryer sheets.

Don't get me wrong. I'm glad she cares. And I'm glad it's Rachel.

But she shouldn't have to do all that. I took care of myself as a human. I can take care of myself as a hawk.

As a boy, I'd been passed back and forth between a much-married aunt and an alcoholic uncle.

And my parents?

Official story: My dad died and my mom walked when I was still too young to remember.

The truth: Yeah, my mom walked out, but the man who died had been my stepfather. I had another father. My real father.

Elfangor.

I found out through a sleazoid lawyer-Controller, of all people. Elfangor had grown tired of war, tired of defending the galaxy.

I knew how he felt. I was defending one small planet, and some days I longed to soar away to some remote mountaintop. Forget the fear and the fighting. Just fly free.

That's what Elfangor did. He flew free. He came to Earth because he was in love with my mother, Loren. He morphed a human man and deliberately stayed past the two-hour time limit — became a *nothlit* — so he could live out his life with her.

He must have believed she was worth it. Personally, I thought he was a little misguided. The only thing I knew about my mother was what my aunt used to tell me . . . and tell me . . . and tell me: "Nutty as a fruitcake and didn't want nothing to do with her own kid. So they dumped you on me."

But Elfangor stayed on Earth for years. Went to college, married my mother, created a life. *Was happy*, I think. *I hope.*

Enter the Ellimist.

The same all-powerful being who'd given me back my morphing powers and left me as a hawk. The Ellimist restored my father's Andalite body, returned him to the Andalite fleet, and erased all memory of him from my mother's mind.

Elfangor fought valiantly in the Andalite war and returned to Earth only once. To save the planet from the Yeerks.

And to die.

Did he know? As he lay in the dirt of that abandoned construction site, his life slipping away, did he know he was talking to his son?

I want to believe he did. To believe I was the reason he trusted me and my friends with his greatest gift.

But the truth is, he was desperate. Once he was gone, the Yeerks would enslave and destroy the planet. And he couldn't let that happen. He probably would've given that morphing ability to any kid who wandered by.

The kid just happened to be me.

I soared over the rooftops and utility lines of the new housing development that had recently popped up near my meadow.

Movement. Steady. Winding. In the yard below. I banked. A snake slid from the grass onto a backyard walkway. Not a rattler this time. An everyday, garden-variety blacksnake. It slithered across the walk, fully exposed.

I circled. The yard was empty, the house dark. The sun was just sinking behind the hills. The streets and houses were draped in shadows. No one would see me.

I circled again. Hunger. Food. Kill. Eat. I swooped. The snake was still alive, still warm, when I ripped into its flesh. Yes. It felt good. It felt hawk. I sank my beak into the meat.

Creeeeeeeeeeeeeek.

I turned my head. The back door of the house inched open. A bare-chested lunatic in camouflage pants darted out, clutching a bow and arrow. Not a toy bow and arrow. This was a compound bow, with weights and sights and a razor-edged arrow fitted onto the bowstring.

The lunatic aimed.

I flapped toward the sky.

Thwwwoooooooooook.

The arrow sliced past. Its feathers raked the edge of my wing. Half an inch to the right, and I would've been birdie shish kebab. I swooped over a row of newly planted trees and dropped down into the next yard.

Thwwwoooooooooook.

Another arrow. Above me. I stayed low, skimming along the spindly line of trees.

A hawk is built to soar, not flap endlessly like a duck. Flying that close to the ground was hard work. No thermals.

But it was my own fault. I knew not to hunt in human territory. In somebody's backyard! It was a stupid mistake. A mistake a real hawk wouldn't have made.

But Tobias the hawk hadn't made the mistake. Tobias the boy had. I'd seen the snake, and my human brain took it as a dare. A snake had stolen my lunch, and now I was stealing it back.

My human brain was going to get my hawk body in big trouble one of these days.

CHAPTER 6

Saturday morning.

I flew to the scoop. I took a longer route this time, bypassing the new housing development. Soared over fields and pastures and circled back to Ax's clearing in the woods.

Ax built his scoop soon after he came to Earth. According to him, it was a smaller version of a typical Andalite home. He'd had to do some remodeling when Marco took up part-time residence with him. Now the scoop was bigger, with a little more enclosed space and a lot more clutter.

Ax was an alien of few possessions. Some research-type books, pictures of his favorite human foods. Some computer equipment. His beloved television set. But Marco was a boy with lots of toys. And he kept a lot of them at the scoop.

The rest of Marco's stuff was at his other home, the cabin he shared with his parents in the Hork-Bajir valley. When we'd rescued Marco's mom, we'd also had to rescue his dad. The Chee helped us stage his — and Marco's — "death." The family evacuated to the valley, and Marco stayed there whenever he could.

But when he needed to be closer to us, closer to the war, he stayed here with Ax.

<How's it going down there?>

<Hello, Tobias.> Ax stood in the open part of the scoop, his stalk eyes scanning the sky. <I am glad you came. We were preparing to find you.>

<Already? You found the site?>

"Complete no-brainer." Marco was hunkered down in front of the computer at the back of the scoop.

I perched on the CD tower behind him.

He leaned back in his chair. "Hospitals, labs, clinics, community blood banks — they all opened right up for us. Kind of scary when you think about it. Your complete medical history is just a click away, available to any nut-job with Internet access. But then we get to this one." He motioned toward the computer screen. "Midtown Bio-Services, Inc. Suddenly it's like breaking into the CIA."

<Actually,> said Ax, <it was far more difficult. We experienced relative ease penetrating the Central Intelligence Agency database.>

<The CIA?> I looked at Marco. <Wait. You hacked into their computer one day for kicks?>

"Hey, the more information we can gather, the better prepared we'll be." He shrugged. "Besides, I gotta have something to do. It gets lonely hangin' here. I almost miss school. Okay. Maybe not. But unless you count the Victoria's Secret Web page, there are no babes in my life anymore."

<There were no babes in your old life,> I said.

"Oh. Very nice, Tobias. Go for the jugular. You've got Rachel tending to your every need. Me, I've got Ax-man." He jerked his thumb toward Ax, who was gazing lovingly at a magazine ad for the new original M&M's. "I'll trade you right now, straight across."

<Yeah, Marco. That'd work.> I glanced at his CD player, satellite dish, and assorted Gameboy cartridges. At the stacks of CDs and the piles of comic books. All of which he'd somehow, mysteriously acquired after having to abandon his old stuff. <You'd make one fine bird of prey.>

He lobbed a *TV Guide* at me.

But you know what? Marco's an opportunist. He would probably adjust to my bizarre version of hawk life better than I had. He'd have no problem with Rachel feeding him. He'd live in her room and wait for her to bring snacks. Preen himself in her mirror all day while she was at school.

Marco wouldn't make himself live by some glorified rule of the hunt, or whatever it was I felt compelled to live by.

<So now what?> I said. <Back to Cassie's barn?>

"Nope." Marco powered the Mac down. "We head straight for this Bio-Services place. It's only a couple of miles from here, and Jake doesn't want to waste time. He thinks a daylight mission on a Saturday morning might catch the Yeerks off guard."

<Off guard?>

"You know what I mean. As off guard as Yeerks ever get. Maybe they won't be expecting us. Maybe we can slip in and out before they notice."

<Yeah, maybe. And maybe you're crazy.>

CHAPTER 7

I caught a nice thermal over the freeway and soared high in the sky. Marco, in osprey morph, stayed behind me, lower and to the side. Ax, the northern harrier, swept back and forth above the rooftops.

We flew over houses and strip malls, parks and ball fields, till we reached the heart of the city. Then we swooped between the downtown skyscrapers. Soared and plunged and emerged over the domed roof of the Civic Center.

The streets around the center had been barricaded with orange sawhorses. Police cars were parked crossways at the corners, lights flashing. Uniformed officers directed traffic away from the them. Eighteen-wheelers, their trailers brightly painted with clowns and tigers, lined the blocked-off streets.

I floated above the big rigs. Below me, burly guys wielding leather prods unloaded elephants from the trailers into a huge pen in the Civic Center's plaza. More policemen tried to hold a crowd of onlookers behind a rope barrier. A monster forklift trundled across the plaza and dumped a huge round bale of hay into a low trough at one end of the pen.

"HhhuuuurrHHHHEEEEEAAAAH!" One of the elephants trumpeted. A dozen others lumbered over to the trough.

Marco swooped out over the plaza. <Hey! How come nobody told me the circus was in town?>

<Jake was afraid you'd try to join it. You know — the whole clown thing?> I circled. <Shouldn't the lab be pretty close?>

<If you bank right, Tobias, and proceed approximately forty-six yards, you should be directly in front of the research facility.>

Ax skimmed over the Civic Center and down a side street. Marco and I followed. Ax was right. It wasn't long before we sailed past a long, low concrete building. A small brass plate beside the door said MIDTOWN BIO-SERVICES, INC. Below it hung a larger sign: NO SOLICITING.

<Gray concrete, no windows, and a complete

lack of architectural charm,> said Marco. <Gotta be Yeerks.>

Cassie, Rachel, and Jake were waiting for us in the alley across the street. We landed, and Marco and Ax demorphed.

"We don't have much to work with," said Jake. "A pair of solid steel doors in front and a loading dock in back."

"Both armed with Gleet BioFilters," said Cassie.

Which we'd expected. It was starting to become standard equipment at all entrances and exits at Yeerk facilities and all entrances to the Yeerk pool. We'd found that out the hard way. The BioFilters were programmed to destroy any life-form whose DNA wasn't entered into the data bank.

Another bit of technology the Yeerks lifted from the Andalites.

<Prince Jake?> Ax trained his stalk eyes on the research lab. <If the control panel is destroyed, the BioFilter will deactivate.> He paused. <Of course, the control panel is located inside the building, and we are on the outside.>

Jake nodded. "Yeah. So we need to create a diversion. A little chaos, and a whole lot of noise." He looked at Rachel. "Any volunteers?"

Rachel smiled her "let's do it" smile. "Elephant?"

Jake nodded, but Rachel had already started to morph.

Her nose and upper lip melded together into a fat, gray nub. Ears sprouted like a pair of gray pot holders. Soon the pot holders were beach towels, the nub a full-fledged trunk. Legs and arms thickened. Hands and feet flattened. Tanned skin dissolved into leathery gray hide.

Jake outlined his plan.

He turned to Rachel. "You know what to do, right?"

<Call a little attention to myself, short-circuit the bio-zapper, and lead any and all pursuers toward the circus, where I can squeeze in among the other elephants and, in the confusion, demorph.>

"And then?"

<Then?> She swished her rope-thin tail.

Jake sighed. "Then mingle into the crowd, do not call attention to yourself, and wait patiently for the rest of us."

<Wait patiently. Right.> She saluted him with her trunk. <I can do that.>

Marco looked at me. "She. Cannot. Do. That."

<No,> I said. <Probably not.>

Rachel stood down beside a Dumpster while the rest of us went fly. Definitely not my favorite morph.

Whooosh!

The ground shot up as I shrank to the size of gravel. Bones dissolved, reemerged as fly exoskeleton. My wings thinned to tissue. Feathers shriveled into tiny fly hairs.

Splooooooot.

Four extra legs sprouted from my chest. A pair of antennae shot from the top of my head. My vision shattered into a thousand pieces.

The morph was complete. And my fly brain had exactly one thought. GARBAGE! POOP! I buzzed into the Dumpster, into the wonderful world of curdled milk and moldy pizza boxes. Four other flies darted around me, savoring the stench and the rot.

<Uh, do you guys think you can get a grip?> Rachel called. My compound eyes pieced together her huge gray face, peering down into the Dumpster. <Ax, I don't even want to know what that is you're standing on.>

<I believe it is a ham and cheese sandwich, putrefied. My fly morph finds it very satisfying.>

<Oh, how gross are you?> Rachel cried. <Can you all please just get out of there before I hurl?>

Cassie laughed. <I didn't know rotten mayonnaise could be so . . . so delicious!>

<You people are sick.> Jake. <Rachel's right. We have someplace else to be.>

Rachel's thought-speak helped guide five flies

the relatively short distance to the research lab. Several minutes later, we lit on the wall above the metal doors. Not a moment too soon.

"HhhhRRRRRRuuuhhh!"

Rachel thundered from the alley, pushing the Dumpster with her wrecking-ball head. Shoved it up across the little strip of grass in front of Midtown Bio-Services, Inc.

CRRRRUUUUNCHHH! WHAM!

Slammed the Dumpster into the concrete wall! Backed up and squashed the trunk of a BMW parked at the curb.

<You've made her a very happy pachyderm,> I told Jake. <It's been weeks since her last car-stomping.>

"HhhRRRuh!" Rachel trumpeted before she wrapped her trunk around a NO PARKING sign and ripped it from the sidewalk. Held it high. Waited.

Bzzzzzzzzzzzzzzzzz.

And the thick steel doors slid open.

CHAPTER 8

"Andalite!"

Human-Controllers streamed from the building.

"Surround it! Don't let it escape!"

Rachel reared up on her hind legs. Controllers dove for cover.

<NOW!> Jake ordered.

With her massive trunk, Rachel hurled the NO PARKING sign like a javelin toward the open doors.

Pop. Pop.

Sparks flew.

A cloud of smoke puffed out from the open doors. The NO PARKING sign clanked to the floor.

A computerized voice droned through the smoke. "Bio. Filter. Deactivated. Immediate. Shutdown. Immediate. Shutdown."

Bzzzzzzzzzzzzzzzzz. The doors began to slide shut.

<Let's go! In! In! In!>

Jake zipped through the doorway. Ax, Marco, and Cassie followed.

I hovered outside. Through broken fly vision, I could see Controllers lunging toward Rachel, surrounding her. She reared, head thrashing.

Bzzzzzzzzzzzzzzzzz.

<NOW, Tobias!>

"HhhhRRRRuuuhhh!" Rachel reared again and swung around. Controllers scattered. Rachel charged down the street.

I spun. The doors were an inch apart. Half an inch. I darted between them. Solid steel brushed the tips of my wings. Halfway through. I could see light beyond. Almost there.

WHAM!

The crash of metal vibrated through my body. The rush of air launched me into space.

<Gee, Tobias, we're glad you could join us,> Marco said as I hurtled past.

<Are you okay?> Cassie.

<Yeah.> I flipped upright. <Fine.>

Four other flies hovered on the ceiling. I buzzed up to join them. And to get my bearings.

We seemed to be in a long hallway. Humans and Hork-Bajir bustled along below us, in and out of offices, carrying folders, pushing carts. I didn't need the fractured flashes of red or the clink of glass tubes to know what the carts carried. Fly senses screamed the answer. Blood. Human blood.

<We're definitely in the right place,> I said.

<Yeah,> Jake agreed, <but we need a more useful morph. Better eyes, at least.>

<Hands would be nice.> Marco.

We hummed along the ceiling, looking for a place to demorph. The long hallway led into another, and another. We finally spotted a darkened door at the end of a corridor and darted under it.

And waited. No sound. No movement. No blood, either. Only the overwhelming stench of floor wax and disinfectant. We spread out and demorphed.

<Uck,> Cassie whispered. <I'm standing in a bucket. And guess what? There's still water in it. At least I hope that's what it is.>

We were crowded into a janitor's closet. Three kids, an Andalite, and a bird. I perched on the edge of the sink. Light from the hall shone through an air vent in the door.

<Hey.> I stared at Marco. <You got a new morphing outfit.>

"What, you just noticed?" He tugged at his bike shorts and tight blue T-shirt.

I leaned over and plucked up a beakful of T-shirt. <Does this remind you of anything?>

"Yeah." He pulled his shirt from my mouth. "It reminds me why I never wanted a pet bird."

<No,> I said. <The color.>

Ax nodded. <It is the color of the Blue Band Hork-Bajir.>

Right. The Blue Bands. Visser One's elite Hork-Bajir guard. Part Green Beret. Part armored car. Pure terror.

We stared at Marco's shirt.

"Whoa." He backed up against a row of metal shelves. "You're looking at me like I'm lunch."

<No,> I said. <We're looking at you like you're a giant armband.>

Cassie rummaged through the shelves and found a utility knife and a roll of duct tape. Marco peeled his shirt off and handed it to Cassie.

"No looking," he warned. "There's no telling what the sight of my naked torso might make you do." Marco turned to me. "I'm lethal at the beach."

Cassie struggled to control a grin. And quickly cut the shirt into wide strips.

Then we went Hork-Bajir. Carefully. Five fully

grown Hork-Bajir have no business huddling in a janitor's closet.

I focused on Ket Halpak, my Hork-Bajir morph.

And felt my feathers harden to leather.

Bones ground and popped.

I shot seven feet in the air.

Thump. <Ouch.>

My head banged into the first-aid kit hung on the wall.

My beak grew wider, longer. My neck slithered out like a snake's.

Thooomp! Thoomp! Horns erupted from my forehead. Talons spread to tyrannosaurus proportions. My tail shot out to twice my height.

SHWOOP! SHWOOP! SHWOOP! SHWOOP! Blades burst from my wrists, elbows, knees, tail.

I was a walking switchblade. Death on two legs.

Crouched in a sink, trying not to fillet my friends.

We wrapped our new blue armbands around our biceps and stuck them down with slivers of duct tape.

<Ready?> Jake eased the door open. <Just act like you belong.> He stepped into the hall.

Marco sauntered after him. <Famous last words.>

Jake led the way back to the main corridor.

The rest of us marched behind him, two by two. Human-Controllers and Hork-Bajir scrambled aside to let us pass. Nobody stopped us. Nobody asked where we were going. Nobody even looked us in the eye.

<We should’ve gotten armbands a long time ago,> Marco said.

We neared the center of the building. The crowd of scurrying lab techs and office workers thinned out. We marched down a nearly empty hall, turned the corner —

— and stopped.

Before us lay a narrow passageway. At the end was another pair of solid metal doors, guarded by an armed Hork-Bajir.

The guard leveled his Dracon beam at us.

<Um,> Marco said. <Think we found their computer?>

CHAPTER 9

Jake strode toward the guard. He pushed the end of the Dracon beam away and pointed at the door.

"OPEN."

The guard hesitated. His gaze flickered toward Jake's armband. Then he aimed the Dracon at Jake's chest.

"Where is pass?"

Hey, nobody ever accused a Hork-Bajir of being eloquent.

"Pass?" Jake turned toward us. He jerked his thumb at the guard. "He wants pass! HA-HA-HA-HA!"

Cassie and Marco laughed. "HA-HA!"

"HA-HA!" I clapped Ax on the shoulder. "HA-HA-HA!"

Ax frowned. "Ha," he said.

Jake whipped his snake head back toward the guard. "Surprise inspection. Heh-heh." His laugh turned menacing. He leaned forward till his beak nearly touched the guard's forehead horn. "Visser One."

The guard swallowed. "Visser One?" He reached back and ran his palm over an entry pad on the wall.

Bzzzzzzzzzzzzzzzzz.

The doors slid open.

Jake snatched the Dracon beam from the guard's hand. He pointed it toward the open doorway. "IN."

The guard backed into the room. We marched after him, across a raised metal floor.

<Whoa.>

Yeah. Marco was right. It looked like Mission Control. An electronic map filled one wall. Little green dots were scattered across it, connected like a web to one large red dot. A tiny orange dot flashed beside the red one. A bank of computers faced the map. Rows of numbers scrolled across their screens.

<Analyzing data,> Ax said unnecessarily.

But other than the computers, the guard, and

us, the room was empty. No human-Controllers. No Hork-Bajir.

Jake motioned toward the door. "Close."

The guard turned and swiped his hand over the entry pad.

Bzzzzzzzzzzzzzzzzz.

Jake raised the Dracon beam. <Sorry.>

He thumped the guard over the head with the butt of the weapon. The guard slumped to the floor.

<Okay, Ax,> he said. <We don't have much time. It won't take the Yeerks long to notice their guard is missing.>

Ax raced to a computer. His clawed Hork-Bajir fingers stumbled over the keyboard. <Prince Jake, my Andalite hands would be better suited for —>

<Demorph. Hurry.>

Ax nodded and began to demorph. Jake stood watch over the guard. Cassie, Marco, and I crossed to the map.

Cassie traced the green dots with her finger. <These must be blood collection sites. And this —> She tapped the big red dot. <This must be where we're standing. See? All the green dots lead here. But what's this?> She pointed to the orange dot.

<Yeerk pool?> Marco guessed.

<Ah. Much better.> Ax's Andalite fingers flew

over the keyboard. <I do not mean to be disparaging toward other species, but Hork-Bajir hands were not designed to —> He stopped. <Prince Jake? We may be too late.>

Four Hork-Bajir stared at him.

<They found a match?>

Ax studied the monitor. <Yes. But I don't think the Yeerks are aware of it yet. This file has not been accessed since the computer analyzed the data. And it is only a partial match.>

<Partial?> Marco circled the computer bank. <What does that mean? They either find animal DNA or they don't, right?>

Ax shook his head. <This is very strange. It indicates a human who has significant family ties with one of the Andalite bandits.> He leaned toward the screen. <But the computer has not yet uncovered the identity of this Andalite bandit.>

<Oh man, Jake.> Cassie closed her eyes. <We overlooked something. Something huge. Our blood is all over the place. Every time we fight these creeps, we bleed. Traces of our human DNA is floating around in all that animal blood. All they have to do is scoop it up and wait for a match.>

Jake nodded. <Or a partial match. Somebody in our family.> He stared at Ax. <Tom?>

<No, Prince Jake.>

Marco leaned over Ax's shoulder. <Uh, Tobias?> He looked up at me. <You may want to see this.>

I crossed to the computer. Ax moved aside so I could see the screen. And the name.

Loren.

<But that's my —> I stopped.

My mother. First name. Last name.

Address.

I stared at the screen. She lived only a few blocks from the three-room shack I'd shared with my uncle. An easy walk. One bus stop.

I looked up at the map. At the flashing orange light. My mother. The light represented my mother.

<Uh-oh.> Cassie's voice pulled me out of my stupor. <Trouble.>

Bzzzzzzzzzzzzzzz.

The doors slid open.

A dozen Hork-Bajir marched into the room. Real Hork-Bajir. Wearing blue armbands.

CHAPTER 10

"You can't escape. So, do us all a favor and don't even try."

A human-Controller pushed through the line of Blue Band Hork-Bajir. Orthopedic shoes squeaked against the metal floor. Reading glasses swung from a chain around her neck. She looked like somebody's grandmother. Wrinkled pink cheeks. A puff of white hair. A lavender cardigan pulled over her flowered dress.

But instead of offering a plate of homemade cookies she trained a Dracon beam on us. And said, "Surrender now, or die."

<Ax,> Jake said in private thought-speak.

<Work fast. Erase Tobias's mother from the database. The Controller won't shoot. She can't risk hitting the computers.>

<Yes, Prince Jake.> Ax's stalk eyes swung from the Controller to Jake, then back to the Controller. His fingers raced over the keyboard.

Jake was still holding the unconscious guard's weapon. He met the human-Controller's gaze and held it, then aimed the Dracon beam at the bank of computers.

The Controller chuckled. "My, my. What a well-thought-out plan. Destroy the database, and I'll have no reason to hold my fire. I'll mow you down. You and your little friends. Visser One will be delighted. The so-called Andalite bandits will be dead, and he'll no longer need to divert time and resources to this project. Go ahead, dear. Pull the trigger."

<Uh, Jake, can I make a suggestion? DON'T SHOOT.>

<Thanks, Marco. I'll take that into consideration.> Jake tightened his grip on the Dracon beam. <Ax? How's it going?>

<Not well, Prince Jake. I have encountered an unexpected second level of security. I can break through, but it will take a few moments.>

<Good. Keep working.> Jake studied the Controller. Then, in public thought-speak, he asked, <Have you counted us?>

The Controller narrowed her eyes. "What do you mean?"

<Are you sure we are all here?> Jake's thought-speak was deeper than usual. More exact, like Ax's. Like an Andalite's. Would it fool her?

Did it matter?

<If I destroy the computer,> he said, <you could kill us. But how many Andalites would still be out there? How many escaped "bandits" would you have to report to Visser One?>

The Controller's face hardened. Her gaze swept to Marco, Ax, me, then Cassie. Then to the map. To the red dot, and the smaller dot beside it.

She froze.

Smiled.

She'd seen the flashing orange dot.

She knew they'd found a match.

She turned to Jake. "Be sensible. Surrender peacefully and you won't be hurt. Much. With your morphing abilities, you'll make excellent host bodies. Much better than this worn-out human I'm living in. In fact, Visser One will be so pleased, he'll probably promote me, and I'll end up in one of your heads. Won't that be cozy?"

<I will die before I become a Controller,> Jake pronounced.

Granny shook her head. "Such a pity. But it's

your choice." She turned toward the Hork-Bajir. "Kill them."

The Blue Bands had been standing at attention. Not moving, not blinking, barely breathing. Now they leaped forward in one precise movement. Like automatic weapons.

Jake whirled and fired.

Tssssssssseeeeeeeeeew!

"AAAAAARRRRGGGGGGGGHHHH!"

Two Hork-Bajir fell, their legs severed at the knees. Blue-green Hork-Bajir blood spilled across the metal floor.

Another Hork-Bajir sprang at Jake. And another.

THUMP!

Jake slammed against the wall. The Dracon beam slid across the floor. Under the computer bank. If I could get it —

SWOOP!

A wrist blade sliced past my chest. I jerked away. Stumbled. A Blue Band kicked. Knocked me back.

WHUMP!

My head bounced against a computer. I slid to the floor. The Blue Band lunged for me. I thrust my arm up.

Blades plunged through skin, muscle, bone.

The Blue Band's eyes glared at me. Dimmed

as his body went limp and he collapsed against my chest. I wrenched my arm blades from his belly.

Around me the battle raged. A forest of Hork-Bajir kicking, leaping, clawing.

<Jake! Behind you.>

<Cassie, watch out!>

Fwwwap! Fwwap-fwwap!

Ax's tail blade struck, and struck again.

But I was cut off from the fighting. For now. The dead Blue Band lay on top of me, concealing me. His blue-green blood oozed over me.

I could see the human-Controller. She circled the perimeter, weapon aimed, still not firing. They'd found a DNA match, and she knew it. She couldn't jeopardize the research. She couldn't shoot.

But I could. I inched toward Jake's fallen weapon. If I could destroy the database . . .

I slid my hand under the computer. It had to be there. It —

Yes! My claws brushed something solid, metal.

<MARCO!>

Cassie screamed. I turned my head.

Marco was pinned between two Blue Bands. His beak had been ripped from his face and lay at his feet in a lake of blood.

One Blue Band held Marco from behind. Pulled Marco's head up and back, leaving his neck exposed.

And the other Blue Band raised his wrist blade above Marco's throat.

CHAPTER 11

I shoved the dead Hork-Bajir from my chest.

The Blue Band spit at Marco. “You die.” Then dropped his wrist blade like a guillotine.

<Marco. Kick. Now!>

I dove. Marco kicked. I hit the Blue Band’s feet as Marco thrust his talons into his gut. The Blue Band plunged backward.

He slammed against the computer bank. His head crashed back onto his tail.

And his own tail blades pierced his skull.

I leaped to my feet.

The other Blue Band was still holding Marco from behind. He jerked Marco back.

Cassie attacked. Elbow blade across the Blue Band’s shoulder.

He spun. “FILTH.” Swung at Cassie.

His other arm was still wrapped around Marco’s throat. I lunged for it. Clamped down. I ripped a beakful of skin and muscle from his forearm.

“AAAAAAAHHHHHH.” The Blue Band released his grip.

Marco tumbled forward and I caught him.

The Blue Band leaped for us.

<NO-O-O-O-O-O!>

Cassie rammed him from the side. Her horns pierced his skin. He toppled over the wall of computers.

Marco sagged against me. Blood gushed from his gaping pit of face.

<Jake,> I called. <Marco’s fading fast.>

<Move toward the doors,> he ordered. <I think we can get out.>

I dragged Marco across the floor, sliding and stumbling through bodies and blood. Cassie covered our rear.

A Hork-Bajir hit the floor.

<Cassie?>

<I’m okay!>

Ax, still locked in bladed combat with two Blue Bands.

Fwwwap! Fwwwap! Fwwwap-fwwwap!

<Prince Jake, I had almost broken the secu-

rity code,> he said. <Thirty seconds more at the keyboard and —>

<Leave it, Ax. Let's go!>

The unconscious Hork-Bajir guard still lay, unmoving, by the door. Jake slid the palm of the guard's hand over the door's entry pad.

The door didn't budge.

He slid the guard's palm over the pad again.

Nothing.

The human-Controller cackled. She was standing beneath the electronic map. "I took the precaution of deleting the guard's DNA from the security database before we entered the room." She aimed the Dracon at Jake. "You're trapped, dearies."

Jake dropped the guard's arm and slid his own palm over the pad. Banged it. Pushed it.

Doubled his fist and punched it.

Nothing. Then . . .

Two thick metal prongs erupted through the doors.

The prongs rose. The doors crumpled open.

"GrrrrrrrOOOOOOOOOOOOOWWWWWWWR!"

Rachel, in grizzly morph, bounded through the opening. Behind her in the passageway sat the monster forklift from the circus, motor rumbling.

<Don't think of it as stolen property,> she told Jake. <Think of it as a really big key.>

<Let's bail!> Jake leaped onto the forklift.

"No!" The human-Controller clattered toward us. Rounded the computer bank and leveled the Dracon.

Thwwwap!

Ax's tail struck. Once. Side of his blade to the side of her head. The Controller dropped to the floor, unconscious.

The remaining Blue Bands lunged at Ax.

"GrrrrrrOOOOOOOOOOOOOWWWWWWWR!"

Rachel batted them with her mammoth grizzly paws.

I lifted Marco. Jake and I hauled him through the front of the forklift. I leaped up after him, turned, and caught a glimpse of the map. The orange light was still blinking.

I pulled Marco out of the forklift, into the passageway. Ax leaped down after us, then Cassie, then Jake. Rachel dropped her thousand-pound grizzly butt into the driver's seat.

Beeeeep. Beeeeep. Beeeeep. Beeeeep.

The forklift backed up. The mangled doors slammed shut, locked into place by the lift's metal prongs.

Rachel barreled down from the forklift. <Let's go, let's go!>

Jake and I each thrust a shoulder under Marco's arms. We bounded down the passageway. Crunched over crumbled Sheetrock, broken glass, blood. Rachel was in the lead, Ax and Cassie at the rear. We didn't bother winding through the hallways. Rachel had plowed a straight shot from the front door to the computer room.

<Marco,> I cried. <Demorph. Demorph!>

<Can't. They'll . . . see me.>

<Doesn't matter anymore!> Jake yelled. <DO IT!>

Marco nodded. And closed his eyes.

<Marco!>

<I'm . . . okay. De . . . morphing.> Dark hair sprouted from his bloody Hork-Bajir head. His leathered skin grew soft. Pale.

"Freeze!"

A human-Controller leaped from a doorway and aimed a pistol at us.

Rachel swatted him like a gnat. He thumped against the wall. The pistol skidded under a flattened desk.

Fwwwap-fwwwap!

Behind me, Cassie and Ax battled a fresh group of Hork-Bajir.

In a group we scrambled over two heaps of steel — the front doors, punctured and ripped from the door frame. Marco, fully human, reached back and grabbed Ax, whose hooves

skittered on the slick metal. Pulled him. Up. Over. Outside!

Rachel heaved the Dumpster in front of the doors. And we sprinted toward the alley.

We morphed as we ran. Cassie, Rachel, and Jake demorphed to human. Marco and Ax, already in their natural forms, morphed harrier and osprey. I demorphed to hawk.

Talons shrank. Feathers grew. Arms sprouted into wings. I flapped. Stumbled. Flapped again. Up. Up. Out of the alley.

I cleared the rooftops and circled back to the lab. Ax and Marco soared beside me.

KUUUUNNNG. KUUUUNNNG.

The Dumpster rocked.

<Hurry, Prince Jake,> said Ax. <The Controllers are escaping.>

The Dumpster tipped. Controllers poured from the building and into the street.

Humans.

Hork-Bajir.

The granny-Controller from the computer room. Dracon beam clutched in her bony hand, she squeezed through the crowd and vaulted toward the alley.

I spun. <Rachel! Cassie! Jake!>

I could see them below. Half human. Half bird.

<Fly,> I said. <Finish morphing in the air. They're on you!>

The granny-Controller darted down the alley.

She stopped. Smiled.

And leveled the Dracon.

"You're dead."

TSSSSEEEEEEEEEWWWWWWWWW!

The alley exploded.

CHAPTER 12

<Rachel?>

I reeled. Smoke and dust coated my wings. My throat. Burned my eyes. Chunks of brick and asphalt hailed down on me.

Pigeons flocked in all directions, and behind me, Marco and Ax circled the lab. But no Jake, no Cassie.

No Rachel.

I flapped. High. Higher. One of the buildings had caught fire. A pillar of black smoke poured into the sky.

Ka-BOOOOOOOOOM!

A second explosion. Ash and debris spewed into the air.

<NO-O-O-O-O-O-O!>

<Tobias?>

Rachel's voice. I whirled.

An eagle, a falcon, and an osprey rose from the smoke.

<Rachel! Are you okay?>

<Yeah. A little singed, but okay.>

<Cassie and I are okay, too,> Jake called. <Let's get out of here.>

We climbed toward the sky. Black smoke billowed out below, between us and the Yeerks. Police cars and fire trucks screamed toward the blast site.

In a loose formation we shot over downtown skyscrapers, then split up and took separate routes back to Cassie's barn.

I circled the city. Circled again. I knew where I wanted to go. But my wings would not fly me there.

I was Tobias the Bird-boy, the *nothlit* who devoured live mice and battled evil aliens. I'd stolen Yeerk spacecraft, raided Yeerk strongholds, and nearly gotten myself adopted by a Yeerk visser. I'd been stabbed and burned and mangled and tortured, and only moments ago got the crap beat out of me by Hork-Bajir that should be working for the WWF.

But I couldn't face my mother. Couldn't even face the roof of her house.

You want pathetic? All those years with my

aunt and uncle, no matter what they said about her, I knew — knew — my mother loved me. She wanted me. Wanted to take care of me. But for some reason she couldn't.

I invented reasons for her. Maybe she'd been wrongfully imprisoned by some tyrannical foreign government. Maybe she'd been shipwrecked on a deserted island. Maybe she'd been relocated in the Witness Protection Program.

Maybe I'd been relocated in the Witness Protection Program.

But not once, not one single time, did I imagine she lived eight blocks from me. That she passed my house every single day. And kept going.

I banked and headed for Cassie's. By the time I flapped into the hayloft, everyone else had arrived and demorphed.

Cassie's dad had stacked hay bales high against one wall. Marco was sitting at the top. I perched on a rafter above him. He nodded at me, then leaned forward, elbows on his knees, and stared at the piece of hay in his hands.

Rachel sat below him. Ax was helping Cassie change the doe's bandage. Jake paced outside the pen.

And except for the scritch and thump of wounded animals, the barn was silent.

I caught Ax's gaze. He gave me his mouthless Andalite smile. Warm. And sad.

Marco broke the silence. "I bet they're backing up their hard drive big time now," he said.

It was a joke. Nobody laughed.

Rachel shook her head. "We really blew it."

"Not we," Jake said. "Me."

Ax looked up from the doe. <Prince Jake, you cannot blame yourself. Even if we had succeeded, if we had erased the data, we would not have stopped Visser One. He would continue to collect blood samples until he discovered another match. It was only a matter of time.>

"Time. Yeah." Jake banged his fist into the side of the pen. Cassie and the doe jumped. "And we just ran out. Why didn't I think this through? No, I had to go for the surprise. In. Out. Before they know we're there. Yeah, that worked. If they didn't have samples of our morph blood before, they do now. We left our DNA all over their computer room. Man." He rubbed his hands over his face. "What was I thinking?"

"You were thinking the longer we waited, the more danger we'd be in." Cassie tore off a piece of adhesive tape. "The more danger our families would be in. And you were right."

"Our families." Jake leaned back against the pen. "They're a bigger target now than before we raided the place. The Yeerks know we're onto them. Once they find a match —" He looked up at me, his face twisted with guilt. "Once they

find a match, they'll move in. Cut off any chance our families have to escape."

Silence.

<Then they must escape before the Yeerks find them.> Ax.

Rachel nodded. "We get them out. Now."

"Can we do that to them?" Cassie looked around the barn. At the animals. Her dad's equipment. His small, steady handwriting on the medical charts. "Can we take away their lives?"

"They'll keep their lives," said Rachel. "That's the point. They'll live. They'll just live somewhere else."

How's this for ironic musing. The Yeerks were looking for humans who were related to human Animorphs, and where did they get the match? From a bird with no family. And then, the very moment I find out I do have a family, a mother, she's snatched away.

Worse than snatched away. The Yeerks had her name. Her address.

And I'd given her away to the Yeerks. I stared out the hayloft door. She couldn't fight them off. Not by herself.

"Tobias."

I turned. Marco was looking at me.

He kept his voice low. "Look, I know what you're doing. Mapping out suicidal rescue missions, right? But you can't go near her. She's bait, okay? They know who she is. They're watching her. Waiting for you. She's probably already a Controller."

<You don't know that.>

"Yeah. I do know that. I lived that. Getting yourself killed won't help her."

I looked away. He was right, of course. He made perfect sense.

But perfect sense left my world a long time ago.

"We knew this day would come," Jake was saying. "We've done everything we can to protect our families. To keep them out of this. Now we've got a decision to make. Go home. Get some sleep. We'll meet back here tomorrow morning and take a vote."

Meeting adjourned. I lifted my wings.

"Tobias. Don't leave." Rachel climbed the stack of hay bales. She stood on the top and rested her chin on my rafter. "Stay at my house tonight. You shouldn't be alone."

<Why not? I've always been alone.> My thought-speak was rougher than I'd intended. <Look, Rachel, thank you. I appreciate it. I do. But there's something I have to . . . see ya.>

She nodded. "I know. I'll leave my window open."

A human boy would've kissed her then.

The hawk-boy flew out of the hayloft toward the city.

CHAPTER 13

I found my old house first. My uncle's dump. He obviously didn't live there anymore. Somebody'd mowed the lawn and painted the garage.

I circled and headed toward my mother's. I didn't think about it. Didn't give my wings a chance to refuse. I just flew. Five blocks down, three across. Over abandoned houses, rusted-out cars, and packed-dirt yards. My old neighborhood was scary. My mother's was worse. If I were human, I'd never set foot there.

I found her street. And her house. Second from the corner, across from a burned-out grocery store. A tiny shack squeezed into a narrow strip of yard with two feet of weeds between it and the shacks on either side. It used to be white, and before that some shade of glow-in-the-dark green. Now it was mainly a few stubborn flecks of paint clinging to bare gray wood.

The doors were closed, the shades pulled. Hey, at least she had shades. The other windows on the block were either boarded-up or covered with old sheets.

I drifted over the house. No sign of Yeerks. No sign of any life-form except a scrawny mutt tied to a clothesline three houses down.

I perched in an elm across the street.

A TV blared in the house below me. The channel changed. Changed again. Pat Sajak gave the wheel a final spin. It landed on the $5000 space, and some idiot bought a vowel.

"Where you think you're going?"

A woman's raspy voice, maybe the remote-happy homeowner's, rumbled into the evening air.

"Out."

A younger voice. Male.

"Oh, yeah?" The woman again. "Who's gonna watch Tiffany?"

"She's your kid. You watch her."

"I got plans."

"Me, too."

Reminded me of the enlightened and stimulating conversations I used to have with my aunt.

The door banged open, and a kid about my age stormed across the porch below me.

"Get back here." The floor groaned. The door banged again. "Ricky Lee, you get your butt back in this house."

Ricky Lee didn't even turn around. He kicked an old couch that was lying by the curb and kept going. I watched him jog two blocks to a 7-Eleven.

I focused on my mother's house.

The setting sun threw purple shadows across the street. A lonely streetlight hummed to life at the corner.

But Loren's house stayed dark. Was she home? Did she work on Saturday nights? Did she even live there anymore?

I caught a breeze and circled above the street. Still no sign of Yeerks. I swooped low over her roof.

Movement inside. Footsteps. Not heavy, like a man's. And not hurried. Cautious almost. Steady. Then a clicking. Click-click-click. Click-click-click. A dog's toenails clicking against the floor.

I listened. No other footsteps. Just one careful woman and a decent-sized dog.

A chain jangled, and the front door swung open. The woman stepped onto the porch with the dog. A German shepherd, wearing some kind of harness with a big, rigid handle. Like a guide dog.

Guide dog? I stared at her. She fumbled with her keys, then turned and felt along the edge of the door. She slid the key into the lock and turned it, using her fingers as a guide. She never looked down.

She was blind.

My mother was blind.

If she was my mother. Okay, so she had the same hair I had. And she was thin, like me. And pale. Like me. And her long, straight nose looked just like mine.

Didn't mean she was my mother. She could be anybody. A friend. A new tenant.

A Controller.

The dog stood still, waiting. She leaned down and scratched his neck. "You're such a good boy, Champ."

Her voice was soft. Steady, like her footsteps. And a little . . . familiar.

Familiar? *Get a grip, Tobias. You do not remember her voice. Even if this is your mother, she left you, abandoned you, before you were old enough to remember anything about her. Her voice is not familiar.*

She straightened up. "Forward," she told Champ.

They stepped off the porch. The woman gripped the handle of the harness in one hand. Champ trotted by her side.

They reached the sidewalk. "Left," she said. They turned.

And that's when I saw them. The scars. Deep gashes, running from the top of her skull to the corner of her mouth. Her right eye twisted downward. Her right ear was a mangled stub. Her hair grew in straggly clumps between the ridges.

She reached the corner and stopped. Champ halted when she did. She waited. Then: "Forward."

They stepped off the curb and crossed the street. The woman never stumbled or hesitated. The dog never left her side. I followed them for six dark blocks. Past the 7-Eleven, past boarded-up houses and vacant lots. They slowed in front of an old brick church. Saint Ann's, according to the wooden sign over the door.

They turned into a dark passageway beside the church and went down a flight of steps leading to the basement. The door at the bottom was propped open by a cement block. They disappeared inside.

I couldn't exactly hurtle in after them. Not in hawk form. I flew to the steeple, morphed fly, and buzzed down the stairway.

Light and noise hit me as I entered the basement. Phones rang. Dozens of people sat around long tables, all talking at once. My fly senses zeroed in on the scent of mildew, coffee, sweaty armpits.

Dog.

I buzzed toward the dog smell. Champ was lying on the floor at the end of one of the tables. He eyed me, but didn't move. His owner sat next to him. Less than a foot from me. I could smell her shampoo.

A phone rang. I heard a click.

"Saint Ann's Crisis Center." Her soft, steady voice. "This is Loren. How can I help?"

Loren. She said Loren. I heard her say Loren. My fly wings nearly stalled out. I landed on the table beside her. Beside Loren.

My mother.

"Take all the time you need," she was saying. "That's what I'm here for."

And she was manning phones at a crisis center.

She was poor, alone, maimed, and blind, and she volunteered at a crisis center.

"Are you feeling better now?" she asked. "Good. I'll be here till midnight if you need to talk some more."

Woooosh!

My fly reflexes hurled me forward.

Thwack!

A slab of plastic smacked against the table behind me. A flyswatter. I shot toward a crack in the ceiling.

"Dang. Missed." A man's voice. "Flies sure are thick tonight."

"Oh, don't be so hard on them." Loren's voice. Warm. Laughing. "They're God's creatures, too, you know."

I inched from my hiding place. Who was this woman? She cared about people in crisis. She cared about her dog. She apparently cared about pesky flies in a church basement.

But she didn't care enough about her son to walk eight blocks for a visit.

I buzzed out of the basement and into the night.

CHAPTER 14

"We got the circus in trouble," Rachel said. "Channel 6 reported a rogue elephant escaped from the Civic Center, ripped up a blood bank, and damaged a gas main that later exploded, wiping out an alley and torching an abandoned warehouse."

Marco shook his head. "Hmmm. And they didn't mention that the blood bank is operated by aliens from another galaxy who are conducting research to help speed up the annihilation of our planet?"

The sun was barely up, but we were already assembled in Cassie's barn. Again. Jake had brought Mr. King, one of the Chee.

"The Chee need to know our plans." Jake looked at us. "Whatever we decide."

Mr. King nodded. "We'll help in any way we can. Information, holograms, shelter. Let us know what you need."

"We need to make it go away." Cassie was sitting on the floor in front of the deer pen. "Can you please, please just make this all go away?"

Mr. King, his hologram at least, smiled. "If we could, we would have. A long, long time ago."

"I know." Cassie leaned back against the pen. "I'm sorry. I'm just very tired. I spent most of the night out here, doing what I could for as long as I could." She waved a hand toward the animals. "Who's going to take care of these guys? If my dad's not here, they have zero chance of survival." She closed her eyes. "My dad. He doesn't have a clue what's coming."

"I know." Rachel smiled ruefully. "I spent last night helping Jordan practice her routine for the all-city gymnastics meet. And you know what? She nailed it. She could win the whole thing. Except she probably won't even get to compete. She was all excited, telling me how their coach got them all matching jackets. And I played along, like it was really going to happen. Like everything was normal."

Normal.

I didn't tell the others what I'd done last

night. That I'd stalked my own mother, and afterward landed my fly body in Saint Ann's steeple and just sat there. I don't even know for how long. Long enough that when I finally came out of my stupor, I was afraid that, yeah, I was still a *nothlit*. But a fly this time.

"I'm just so tired of lying to everybody," Jake said wearily. "This morning at breakfast we're all sitting around looking at sale ads in the paper. My mom and dad wanted to go look at a new lawn mower. Tom even said he'd go along. They wanted me to go, like a real family outing. But I made up a story about having to help Cassie's dad here at the farm."

"It wasn't exactly a lie." Cassie.

"It wasn't exactly the truth, either." Jake shook his head. "My mom doesn't understand why I never have time for them anymore. At least if we do this, if we get them out, that part will be over. Lying. Sneaking around. Hurting their feelings." He let out a breath. "But we came here to vote, so let's do it. Rachel?"

"I'm in."

"Cassie?"

"What choice do we have?"

"Marco?"

"We do it. Definitely."

"Ax?"

<I do what you do, Prince Jake.>

"I vote yes. But . . ." Jake looked at us. "I'm taking Tom." It wasn't a question. "I know it's a risk, but I think it's a containable risk. My parents won't leave him behind. I won't leave him behind. So, as long as everybody understands that, I vote yes."

<I understand, Prince Jake.>

"Tom's part of the deal," said Rachel.

Cassie and Marco nodded.

"Tobias?" Jake looked up at me. "You haven't voted."

<We get them out,> I said. <All of them.>

All of them. But I'm not sure Jake understood me.

He rubbed his temples. "Okay. Decision made. They'll be safest in the new Hork-Bajir valley. Marco's parents are already there. And the Yeerks think they destroyed it. We'll take my family last. That way if anything goes wrong with Tom, everybody else will already be safe. We'll have to watch them, guard them, for the first three days. To make sure none of them are Controllers. And to make sure . . ."

<To make sure the Yeerk in Tom's head dies,> Ax said, in his usual blunt way.

"Right." Jake nodded. "We'll all be living with the Hork-Bajir, too. We can't stay down here in the city. Too dangerous. The Yeerks would be all over us."

"So. We pack our toothbrushes and run."

"No, Rachel. We retreat," Jake answered. "A tactical retreat. Save the army. Live to fight another day. But a toothbrush would be good. And extra deodorant. We'll be out there a while."

<The Yeerks have probably already mobilized,> said Mr. King. <I suggest you begin the evacuation soon.>

"How about now?" Cassie stood and brushed the hay from her jeans. "My parents are both home, which almost never happens. Let's do it."

CHAPTER 15

Cassie eased open the barn door. Her mom was on the porch, drinking coffee and reading the Sunday paper.

"My parents are scientists," Cassie said quietly. "They believe in logic and reason, backed by hard evidence. We have to show them proof and explain it all rationally, or they'll never buy it."

Mr. King created a hologram of Cassie's porch, barn, and yard. To anyone outside the hologram — driving by, flying overhead, lurking in the bushes — it looked like Cassie's mom was still sitting alone at the porch table, absorbed in world news.

Inside the hologram, I flew across the yard

and landed next to her coffee cup. She didn't look up.

Clink-clink. I tapped my beak on the cup.

She peered over the top of her paper. "My. Aren't you a friendly hawk."

<Sometimes,> I said. <Although Yeerks and small rodents might disagree.>

She stared at me. "Oooooo-kay." Shook her head and raised the paper back up in front of her eyes. "I did not hear that."

<Not with your ears,> I said. <I'm speaking to your mind.>

Silence. Cassie's mom didn't move for a full minute.

Then she carefully lowered the paper, folded it into a neat rectangle, and reached for her cup. "Coffee. I definitely need more coffee, because I'm still dreaming." She scooted her chair back. "I knew we shouldn't have switched to decaf."

"It's not the coffee, Mom."

Cassie, Rachel, Marco, and Jake had slipped across the yard while Cassie's mom and I were chatting. Rachel, Marco, and Jake took positions around the yard.

"What on Earth is going on?"

Cassie climbed the steps to the porch. She opened the kitchen door and poked her head inside. "Daddy? Can you come out here?" Then she

turned to face her mother. "You're not dreaming, Mom. Tobias isn't a normal hawk."

Her mother looked at me. "You got that right."

"He's a human in hawk form," Cassie went on patiently, like she was explaining a very complicated concept to a very young and innocent child. "He's communicating through thought-speak. It's like telepathy."

"Telepathy. Uh-huh." Her mother crossed her arms and leaned back in her chair. "What kind of game are you and your friends playing, Cassie? Do you have a hidden microphone somewhere?" She glanced at the row of flowerpots behind her. "Are you taping this, me acting the fool?"

Cassie's voice remained admirably calm. "We're not taping anything, Mom, and it's not a game." She looked at me and nodded.

I focused on Tobias the boy. My feathers began melting to human skin.

"Look, Cassie, this is my first day off in a very long time, and I'm trying to enjoy — oh!" Cassie's mom had caught sight of my swirling, brown-and-tan feather-skin.

"Something's wrong with that bird! Get back, Cassie."

Before I could stumble away, she threw the sports section over me, wrapped me up, and scooped me under her arm.

"There's nothing wrong with him, Mom," Cassie said. Okay, now there was slight panic in her tone. "Put him down."

Pop. Pop. Pop. Pop. Pop. Fingers shot from the ends of my wings.

"Good heavens." Cassie's mom stared at the human hands hanging out beneath the newspaper wrapping. "Cassie, get your father. Tell him to meet me in the barn. In the operating room. Stay back, all of you. It could be contagious."

"Mom, wait!"

Cassie's mother bounded down the porch steps, with me still growing heavier and taller, under her arm.

That's when Ax ambled toward us across the yard.

"Ahh!"

THUNK!

I fell to the ground. My beak melted into a human nose and mouth. Talons stretched into human feet, and I was a boy. A boy lying on his head in the dirt. I sat up.

Ax turned his stalk eyes toward me. <Is she a Controller?> he asked privately.

<I can't tell,> I answered. <But I don't think so.>

Cassie's mom slowly, slowly backed up the steps, her arms held out to her sides, barring Cassie from coming down from the porch.

"Get back, Cassie." She kept her eyes on Ax. Her body between her daughter and the blue creature. "I knew those high voltage power lines would have an impact on the wildlife. Stay behind me. It could be radioactive."

"He's not radioactive, Mom." Cassie pushed past her mother and came to stand beside Ax. "He's just a very long way from home."

Cassie's mother continued to stare at Ax. Then at me. The sports page was still wrapped around my leg.

She narrowed her eyes. "You were a hawk. I can't believe I'm saying this, but a few minutes ago you were a hawk."

I nodded.

She looked at Ax. "And he . . . ?"

"Is an Andalite," Cassie said softly. "His name is Aximili-Esgarrouth-Isthill. We call him Ax. He's our friend."

Ax stepped forward and bowed.

<It is a pleasure to make your acquaintance, Mrs. Cassie's Mother.>

"Uh, yes. You, too." Her eyes shifted back to her daughter. "An Andalite? He's talking in my head, too." Then she looked back to Ax. Inched toward him. Circled him. "And he's supposed to look like this?"

Cassie nodded. Ax frowned.

"Amazing." Cassie's mom reached out and ran her hand across the blue fur on Ax's rump.

"Mom!" Cassie snatched her mother's hand away. "Would you play with Jake's butt?"

"Of course not!"

"Then quit playing with Ax's!"

CHAPTER 16

"Hey." The kitchen door slid open. Cassie's father stumbled out onto the porch, clutching a coffee mug in both hands. "I want to know whose brilliant idea it was to schedule sunrise at — whoa."

He stared at Ax. Rubbed his eyes and stared again. Frowned and peered down into his mug.

"It's not the coffee, Walter."

"Sit down," Cassie said. "Both of you." She led her mother up onto the porch and planted both her parents in chairs.

And then she did an amazing impression of a wolf.

Her skin sprouted thick gray fur. Ears shifted upward and elongated. Her small Cassie nose shot out into a wolf's sensitive snout.

And her parents watched, stunned.

<I'm okay.> Cassie dropped to all fours. <I'm still me. But for a while I'm also a wolf.>

As she finished the morph, she told them about the Yeerks. About Visser One and Elfangor. About Marco's parents. And Tom. She explained morphing technology and our battle to save Earth.

And then she morphed back.

Her mother scooped her into her lap. "Baby. Oh, my baby." She stroked Cassie's hair and kissed her face, over and over.

Her father wrapped his arms around them both. "Why didn't you tell us, Cassie? We could've helped."

"I wanted to keep you safe. For as long as possible." Cassie shook her head. "But I can't anymore. The Yeerks are closing in. We have to leave. You. Me. All of us. Now."

"Now?" Her mother held Cassie's face between her hands. "Baby, I can't just leave my job, my house, and go running off to who knows where. I have responsibilities."

"No, Mom. You don't. You only have your life and your family. And if you stay here, you'll lose them both." Cassie turned to her father. "Daddy, you believe me, don't you?"

"I believe you, Cassie, but your mother's right. We can't just leave. Too many people, too many animals depend on us."

"No," Cassie repeated firmly. "Not anymore. You don't understand."

"Perhaps I can help." Mr. King seemed suddenly to appear. He'd dropped his human hologram and stood before us in his true metal-and-ivory, vaguely canine android form.

"Good Lord." Cassie's mom put her hand to her head. "What else is stashed in our barn?"

Mr. King maintained the large hologram of Cassie's yard and barn. But inside it he projected another hologram, one only those of us on the porch could see. A 3-D movie of one of our old battles. Images flashed. Cassie, in wolf morph, mangled and bleeding. A human-Controller, a cop, firing on her. Cassie jerking. Falling. Lying in a bloody, lifeless heap.

The images stopped.

For a moment there was silence.

Then Cassie's dad spoke. "We need to leave," he said. "Now."

His wife nodded.

We waited while the family prepared to leave. Cassie's dad dragged their camping equipment from the garage. Her mom packed some suitcases. Cassie threw her things in her backpack. Before she slid the backpack in the family's truck, she pulled something out so we could see. It looked like one of those square picture-frame/paperweight things. The morphing cube, its blue surface hidden by photos.

Then we helped Cassie's dad load the smaller animal cages into the truck.

Cassie fed the doe, then stood by the pen, stroking the deer's neck. "I don't know what to do. She's too big to take with us, and I can't come back here to take care of her."

"Don't worry." Mr. King lifted an opossum cage and headed toward the truck. Cassie reluctantly followed. "I was Louis Pasteur's lab assistant in a former incarnation. I was actually the one who suggested heat as a way to kill bacteria. I'll look in on the doe, feed her, change her bandages. And when she's able, I'll lead her to safety."

"Thank you." Cassie squeezed his android hand and slid into the cab of the truck with her parents.

Marco morphed gorilla and leaped into the back. He hunkered down between the opossum cage and a pile of lawn chairs. <Think of me as a furry guardian angel,> he said and Cassie's mom gave him a look.

Mr. King extended his hologram to cover the road in front of Cassie's house. We watched the truck rumble away.

Rachel sighed. "My house next. And it won't be pretty."

CHAPTER 17

<Logic and reason won't work here,> Rachel coached. <My mom's a lawyer. There's no arguing with her. She'll win, whether she's right or not. We just have to do what we came for.>

We'd flown to Rachel's house in our various bird-of-prey morphs. Lourdes, another Chee, was waiting for us on the porch. Rachel, Jake, and Ax demorphed, and Rachel led us inside.

We crowded into the front hall. *CatDog* blasted from a TV in the living room. A woman's voice drifted through the kitchen doorway.

Rachel rolled her eyes. "My mom. On a business call. Exactly where she was when I left this morning. By now her cell phone is probably vacuum-sealed to her ear."

We crept toward the kitchen. Rachel's sisters were lying on the living room floor in their pajamas. Too busy eating Pop-Tarts and watching TV to notice their sister, their cousin, an alien, and a red-tailed hawk slip past.

Amazing, a kid's capacity to ignore the bizarre.

Ax guarded the living room door. I perched on a coatrack where I had a good view of Rachel's mom pacing the kitchen. Rachel and Jake tiptoed upstairs. They returned a few minutes later carrying three suitcases and a Barbie overnight bag.

Rachel morphed grizzly. Jake crossed through the kitchen and positioned himself in front of the sliding glass doors.

"We've rescheduled this deposition twice," Rachel's mom spat into the phone. "We're not doing it again."

She looked up, saw Jake, and frowned. Where's Rachel? she mouthed.

Jake pointed toward the hall. Rachel's mom nodded, turned and paced the other way.

"Look, Harold, my client has been . . . it doesn't matter. No. NO! We're going ahead with it tomorrow as planned."

She slammed the phone shut and rubbed her temples.

Rachel lumbered into the kitchen. I flew in behind her and landed on top of the refrigerator.

<You probably should've let them reschedule, Mom. Tomorrow isn't going to be good for you.>

Her mother whirled. Backed up until she hit the wall. "Wha —? Rachel, where are you? Jake, run! Go around front and get Sara and Jordan. Girls! Get out of the house!"

"Sara and Jordan are fine, Aunt Naomi," Jake said, in his talking-to-psycho-relatives voice. "And so are you. Ax?" He raised his voice, but kept it calm. "Can you make sure Rachel's sisters don't go anywhere?"

Little girl giggles erupted from the living room.

<I have already made sure, Prince Jake. They think I am a "pokey man." I have told them I am an Andalite and am actually quite swift, but they insist they need to train me.>

Ax clopped into the kitchen with Sara on his back. Jordan paced along behind.

"My babies! Leave them alone!" Rachel's mom reached behind her and ripped a spice rack from the wall. And lunged at Rachel.

Yes, lunged at a grizzly bear. With a spice rack.

I was amazed. Cassie's mom had done the same thing. Thrown her own body between her child and what she believed was a mutant, radioactive deer.

This is what mothers did. This is how they acted. They put themselves in danger to save their kids.

<Oh, right, Mom.> Rachel held her mother back with one paw. <You're really gonna do some damage with the bay leaves?>

"Rachel? I hear you!" Her mother collapsed against the bear. Pressed her ear against Rachel's grizzly belly. "Are you in there? My God, this creature ate you alive."

<Oh, brother.> Rachel rolled her squinty bear eyes. <Mom, listen to me. I'm not in the bear. I am the bear. Get a grip. You have to drive.> She heaved her mother over her shoulder. <Jordan, grab Mom's purse.>

Jordan nodded and snatched a huge leather bag from the kitchen counter.

Like I said before, it's amazing, a kid's capacity to accept the bizarre.

Rachel bounded across the kitchen and ripped open the door to the garage. Ax herded Jordan and Sara out after her. Jake gathered their suitcases and followed. I brought up the rear.

Rachel dumped her mom onto the driver's seat. Her sisters scrambled into the back.

<Just relax, everyone.> Rachel, still in grizzly morph, squeezed into the front passenger seat.

There was some damage. <I'll explain as we go. We all need a vacation, and I have a feeling this is going to be a long one.>

"How long?" Jordan frowned. "We have to call Daddy. How will he find us?"

Rachel didn't answer for a moment. Then, in gentle thought-speak — gentle for Rachel — she said, <Don't worry about Daddy. I'll tell him. He'll find us. I promise.>

She punched the remote, and the garage door rumbled open.

<I've got this one covered,> she told Jake. <You need Ax and Tobias with you.> She turned to her mother. <Let's do it.>

Her mom started the car, threw it in reverse, and screeched out of the garage. I think she was very ticked. At the end of the drive the car spun. Then it lurched forward, and they sped away.

Lourdes's hologram masked their exit.

We watched to make sure no one followed them. Then Jake and Ax morphed wings, and we flew to the next house.

Jake's.

And Tom's.

CHAPTER 18

<We take Tom first,> Jake said. <No explanation. No discussion. Just grab him. Give him zero time to react. It shouldn't be hard. He can't fight all three of us. Once we have Tom, my parents will come willingly. They won't let us kidnap Tom without them.>

Of course they wouldn't. They'd risk anything to save him.

That's what parents did.

We circled above Jake's house. A hawk, a harrier, and a falcon, looking for signs of alien activity. Jake was focused, the way he always is. Serious. Determined. All the normal Jake stuff, maybe edged up a notch or two.

But he also seemed, I don't know, fearless.

Defiant. His turns were a little sharper, his dives a little steeper. Almost like a fighter pilot. Almost like Rachel.

I watched him sweep over his neighborhood, spin, and plummet toward his house. Yeah, we were taking his parents. Forcing them to leave everything they knew, everything they loved.

But we were also taking Tom, and it was the moment Jake had been waiting for since this war began. The moment when he would liberate his brother from the Yeerks. The moment Jake would finally set the real Tom free.

We landed behind a row of shrubs.

Erek was waiting for us. "Nobody's home," he told us. "I came here right after you called, and the house was empty. I haven't seen a soul since."

Jake nodded. <They went shopping. I thought they'd be home by now. But that's okay. When they get here, they'll already be in the car. All three of them. They'll pull into the driveway. Erek, you cloak the place in a hologram. Ax, Tobias, and I jump in, pin Tom down, and force my dad to drive away. This is good. Makes our job simple.>

Simple. Right.

Jake and Ax demorphed. Ax stayed hidden in the bushes. Jake unlocked the front door and slipped inside. I took to the sky. Still no sign of Yeerks. And no sign of Jake's parents.

The garage door slid open. Jake stood inside, surrounded by a pile of bulging suitcases and other items he thought his family would need. His mom's laptop. His dad's golf clubs. Tom's basketball.

He scooted it all out into the bushes and closed the garage door. The ball rolled down the driveway. Jake ran after it.

<Prince Jake.> Ax's stalk eyes scanned the street. <The longer they are gone, the more worried I become.>

<I'm with Ax.> I floated above the house. <We're leaving a trail. Cassie's farm. Rachel's house. It won't take the Yeerks long to find out the families are gone. And even less time to figure out your family's next.>

"They'll be home." Jake dribbled back up the drive, toward the basketball hoop mounted above the garage door. "It'll take my dad a while to decide on a lawn mower."

<Lawn mower,> I repeated.

"Yeah."

<With Tom.>

"Yeah."

<Okay, think about this a minute. Tom is a fairly high-ranking Controller. By now he knows

about the blood bank break-in. About a partial human DNA match. But he's spending the morning shopping for a lawn mower. Does that strike you as odd?>

"No." Jake faked left, broke right, charged the basket. "Lawn mowers are on sale. They went to look at them. Perfectly normal." He shot. "A family looking at lawn mowers."

Swish! Through the net.

Jake loped toward the garage and grabbed the rebound. "Nothing odd about it."

I climbed higher. Scanned the grid of streets. Below me I heard the steady *th-thump* of the basketball bouncing against the garage door.

"Do you see them?" Erek asked.

<No,> I said. <Nothing.>

Th-thump. Th-thump.

<Prince Jake?> Ax again. <Tom is infested with a ruthless, power-hungry Yeerk. And your parents —>

"I know, Ax." Jake slammed the basketball against the garage door. "I know. My parents aren't safe with him. He tried to infest my dad with a Yeerk. He tried to . . . he tried to . . ."

Kill him. Tom the Controller had tried to kill his own father.

Th-thump. Th-thump.

Movement. A flash of silver in the distance. I circled.

<I see them. Three blocks away, headed for your house.>

The thumping stopped. "All of them? Is Tom still with them? My mom. My dad. Are they okay?"

<They're all inside. And they're all okay. But —>

"But what?" Jake yelled.

I banked. Two SUVs were keeping pace with their car on parallel streets.

<It's a trap, Jake. The Yeerks are onto us. We have to get out of here. Abort the mission.>

"I can't leave, Tobias! They're my family."

<Prince Jake, remember. Tactical retreat. Save the army. Live to fight another day.>

"No! There won't be another day. If we don't get them out now, we may not get another chance."

Jake dropped the basketball. Orange-and-black stripes erupted from his skin. Tiger fur.

His parents' car sped up. So did the SUVs.

I dove. Rocketed toward the car. I had no idea what I was doing. A lone hawk against a Lexus. Maybe I could get Jake's dad's attention. Turn him around. Get him to stop. Something.

I flew low and hard. Swooped past the passenger door.

The window rolled down. I caught a glimpse of Jake's mom. Her face, hard and twisted. Her hand, clenched. A glint of metal.

I spun.

Tsssseeeeeeeeeeeeeeeeeew!

Dracon fire blasted past. The neighbor's bird-bath exploded. I reeled. Choked on the stench of burned feathers. I flapped. The tips of my wings were singed.

Jake's mom leaned from the car. She turned. Aimed.

I swept toward the sky. I could see Tom through the rear window. He reached over the backseat. Slapped the Dracon beam from his mother's hand. It bounced across the pavement.

Tsssseeeeeeeeeeeeeeeeeew!

A black scar ripped across the front of Jake's house.

It seemed like an omen.

CHAPTER 19

<Prince Jake! We must retreat.> Ax had already begun to morph. Feathers sprouted from his blue fur.

One of the SUVs barreled out of a side street. The Lexus swerved. Jumped the curve. Leveled a row of mailboxes, then veered back onto the street. Past Jake's house. Past the drive. Jake's dad jerked the steering wheel. The car spun. Gravel sprayed over the neighbor's yard.

<Get out of there, Jake!>

Ax flapped up from the bushes. <Now, Prince Jake!>

"There's nothing more you can do here," Erek added.

Jake nodded. The black-and-orange stripes

had already disappeared. The feather pattern of a peregrine falcon began to etch itself across his skin.

The car's engine revved. The Lexus lurched forward.

"Jake, wait!" Erek cried. "I'll project a hologram to hide the morph."

"No. I want them to see this."

In full view of his family, Jake morphed a peregrine falcon. His body shrank. Arms became wings. Feet became talons.

<This is for them.> His thought-speak was a whisper. <For my real family. To give them hope and, finally, the truth. And for their Yeerk captors. To give them warning.>

The car slammed into the driveway. Jake's mom leaped from the front seat and bolted across the yard. Toward the Dracon beam that had bounced into the grass.

<Jake, NOW!> I turned. Plummeted toward the weapon.

Jake lifted his wings and rose above the driveway.

His mom dove for the weapon. Rolled. Aimed.

I hurtled toward her. Raked her arms with my talons.

Tsssseeeeeeeeeeeeeeeew!

Jake's bedroom window shattered. Jake swooped over the roof. Ax followed.

"Filthy humans!" Jake's mother screamed.

The two SUVs screeched into the driveway. Controllers raced across the lawn.

"Fire at will. They will not escape!"

I spun. Powered my wings. Circled the house.

Bushes exploded around me. Twigs pelted my wings.

I rounded the corner into the backyard. Jake and Ax were waiting. We shot around the house behind Jake's. Crossed the next street, darted between the next row of houses, then the next. Controllers chased us, but airborne raptors are faster than humans on foot. The shouts and blasts faded away.

We shot out of the residential neighborhood and swooped over the mall. The sun radiating off cement and asphalt created a beautiful thermal. I spread my wings. They were numb from endless flapping. Ax spread his, too. Warm air billowed under us. We jetted toward the clouds.

But Jake flapped on. Low and straight ahead. He swept over the mall and out over the interstate. Buzzed an eighteen-wheeler. Rocketed through a web of power lines. Shot beneath an underpass. Flapped and soared. In and out of traffic.

<This was not your fault, Prince Jake,> Ax called from above. <You could not have known

what Tom was planning. You could not have stopped him.>

Jake's thought-speak was bitter.

<Yeah, Ax. I could have.>

Jake spun sideways and shot between two signposts.

Then spread his wings and rose. <What's wrong with me? Why didn't I get them out last night? When I need to wait, plan, gather more information, what do I do? Charge in. Go for the surprise. Screw things up permanently. But when I need to charge in, to save the people I love most, I wait. I say, "Go home. Get some rest. Sleep on it." Great plan. I get sleep. My parents get Yeerks.>

He swept out ahead of us. Climbed high above a strip mall. We stayed with him.

<We will return, Prince Jake. When the time is right, we will get them out.>

Jake dove. Hurtled toward Earth at two hundred miles an hour. Toward the parking lot below. He pulled up seconds before his beak hit pavement, skimmed along the asphalt, and climbed again.

Jake, our fearless leader. On a crazed kamikaze mission.

I'd never seen him like this. Even in our lowest moments, he'd always been steady. Resolute.

He weighed the costs, made a decision, forged ahead.

And I'd always wondered how he did it. How he kept it straight in his mind. Yeerks. Visser One. Aliens conquering humans, conquering the planet. Fighting the enemy without becoming like them. How did he sort through all that? The emotions, the ethical dilemmas, the moral crises? How did he wrap his brain around it all so he could make logical decisions? Smart decisions. The kind that saved the lives of his team. The kind that set the enemy back a small step or two.

But now I knew. Jake didn't understand any of it any better than the rest of us did. If he defeated the Yeerks, freed humanity, rescued Earth, that was good. But that was a bonus. His main goal was much simpler. To save his family. That goal was what had given him strength. That goal was what had kept him sane. Allowed him to retain a center of calm focus amid the awful chaos.

Family.

The houses below us thinned out. Shopping areas rippled into foothills.

<I need to hunt,> I said. <Catch up with you later.>

I peeled off and soared toward my meadow. Jake and Ax disappeared over a ridge.

I banked and flew back into the city.

CHAPTER 20

I floated above the roof. Her windows were open a crack. The window shades banged in the breeze.

Noises drifted out. Her footsteps. Her voice. "Hungry, boy? There you go, my big sweetheart."

Paper rustled, like a bag opening. Then a muffled clatter. Dog food tumbling into a dish. Toenails skittered across the floor.

Champ was eating lunch. Which meant he and Loren probably weren't going anywhere soon.

Not a problem. I could wait.

But I wouldn't be waiting alone. The Yeerks had sent a welcoming committee.

A bag lady pushed her cart along the sidewalk

in front of Loren's house. She reached the corner, turned around, and pushed it back.

An old van sat across the street, in the vacant lot between Ricky Lee's house and the boarded-up grocery store. It was wrapped in vines and cobwebs, and nearly swallowed by weeds, as if it had been abandoned in that spot years ago.

But it hadn't been there yesterday.

On the next corner, a teenager lounged at a bus stop. He tried to look casual, jamming to his CD player. His shoulders bobbed. His size-thirteen Reeboks thumped against the concrete. But his eyes were fixed on Loren's house. A bus pulled up. Pulled away. The kid didn't budge.

I drifted over the street. My shadow floated across the sidewalk below me. The bag lady stared at it. Glanced up. Watched me for just a moment too long. Her gaze flicked to the abandoned van. She mumbled something into her shopping cart.

My hawk ears picked up bits of it: ". . . above the house . . . can't tell . . . don't want to draw attention . . . wait . . . see if it . . ."

I soared down the street, away from Loren's house. I swooped and glided, in complete view of the bag lady and the van and the kid at the bus stop. Just like a normal hawk on a sunny afternoon. I swept over a billboard three blocks away and dropped down behind it, out of sight.

I waited. Nothing. I skimmed along the sidewalk, circled the neighborhood, and approached Ricky Lee's house from behind.

I perched on a fence post by the alley. Still nothing.

I soared across the backyard, careful to stay out of sight of the van, and flapped up onto the roof.

I stayed just below the roofline on the backyard side, hidden between the chimney and a TV antenna. Ricky Lee was home, watching a *Brady Bunch* marathon on Nickelodeon. I dug my talons into the tar shingles and waited.

I could see Loren's house. And the bag lady, who'd pushed her cart to the corner again. She gazed at the sky, in the direction I'd flown, frowned, and pushed her cart back the other way. At the bus stop, the teenage kid was still jamming under his headphones. And still watching Loren's house.

For hours. The shingles softened in the afternoon sun. My talons sank deeper. The bag lady sat down on the curb. The kid with the CD player sat through twelve buses.

And still, Loren stayed inside.

What was she doing in there? How did a blind woman occupy her time, all day long, all by herself?

Another bus rumbled up. Rumbled off. Finally Loren's door swung open. She and Champ stepped out onto the porch.

The bag lady leaped to her feet. The kid at the bus froze in mid-jam. I wrenched my talons from the tar and swooped across Ricky Lee's backyard toward the alley. I stayed low. Circled the block.

Loren and Champ set out in the direction of the church. The bag lady and her cart rattled along behind, at a distance. I followed, flitting between backyards, below rooflines.

They crossed the street.

<The dog, man. The dog's your ticket.>

Marco's thought-speak. I banked. An osprey and a northern harrier jetted up behind me. Marco and Ax.

<What are you guys doing here?>

<Protecting an endangered species,> Marco replied. <You.>

<Prince Jake sent us. He thought you might need help. I remembered the address.>

We floated another block. Past the bus stop. Loren and Champ stopped at the corner, turned, and crossed the street toward us. Toward the 7-Eleven. They navigated the parking lot and disappeared inside.

Ax, Marco, and I landed in the Dumpster

behind the store. Ax and I went human, Marco demorphed, and we crept around the building.

The bag lady had stopped across the street. She leaned on her shopping cart and watched the store.

"Casual," said Marco. "Just act casual. We're three neighborhood punks hanging at the 7-Eleven."

He strutted toward the door. Ax and I followed.

CHAPTER 21

The place was nearly empty. An old woman flipped through a *National Enquirer* at the front. Two little boys fingered the candy bars next to her. Loren was on the other side of the store, in the meager grocery section, making her way down one of the aisles. A lone cashier manned the counter.

Ax sidled up to him. "Do not worry," he said. "We are irresponsible teenage hoodlums, possibly gang members, but you are not in any danger."

The guy gave Ax a blank stare.

"His gang's from out of town," I explained.

Marco grabbed Ax's shirt and pulled him toward the back of the store. "Smooth, Ax-man. That'll look real convincing on the surveillance tapes."

We jostled past Loren and Champ.

"Man, take your dog outside," Marco drawled. "He stinks."

Loren didn't say a word. Just kept her steady pace. She felt along the top shelf till her fingers touched a box of Raisin Bran. She picked it up, shook it, and placed it in the shopping basket on her arm.

I watched her. My mother. She did her grocery shopping at a convenience store. But I guess she didn't have much choice. The neighborhood wasn't exactly brimming with bright, shiny Safeways.

"Hey, you big mutt," Marco called to Champ. "Want a drink?" He picked up a supersize cup and filled it. Coke sprayed onto the floor.

Champ ignored him. So did Loren. She crossed to the coolers along the back wall, pulled out a quart of milk, and placed it in her basket. I could see the date stamped on the lid. The milk had expired three days ago.

"Isn't that sweet?" I jerked the basket from her hand. "She's buying us a little snack." I slid the milk out of the basket and replaced it with a fresh quart from the cooler. "Man. Nothing but cereal and dog biscuits." I shoved the basket back in her hand. "Keep it, lady."

She didn't say anything. Didn't hesitate. Just ran her fingers along the cooler doors — counting them, I think — opened one, and pulled out a package of bologna. She turned and started back up another aisle. We followed.

"She does not seem to be afraid of us," Ax whispered.

"She's probably been through worse," I said tightly.

"Ah." Ax nodded. "She does not understand how menacing we are." He tapped her on the shoulder. "You do not know me," he said, "but I am a juvenile delinquent. I do not trust authority figures, I probably will not graduate from high school, and statistics say my present rowdiness and vandalism will likely lead to more serious crimes. I am a dangerous fellow, and I am causing mayhem in this store."

He reached behind her and pulled three jars of baby food from the top shelf. Shoved them behind a box of macaroni. Shuffled the Cheez Whiz in front of the Marshmallow Fluff. Tossed a bag of lady's shavers onto a bag of hamburger buns.

"There. I have now shamelessly destroyed the symmetry of this shelf, undoing hours of labor by underpaid store employees. If you could see me, you would be frightened."

"If she could see you, she'd have you committed," Marco muttered. He grabbed the handle of Champ's halter and jerked it from Loren's hand. "Listen, lady, we're gonna borrow your dog."

He pulled on the harness. Champ planted his paws. Marco tugged. Champ tugged back.

"Oh, brother." Marco placed his hand on Champ's head.

Immediately Champ relaxed. His alert brown eyes dimmed. His shoulders sagged. The dog had fallen into the acquiring trance. Marco kept his hand on Champ's head and pulled on the harness. Champ meekly stepped toward him.

"Don't go anywhere," Marco told Loren. "And don't call the cops or Fido here gets it."

He led Champ through a door marked PERSONNEL ONLY. Ax and I followed. It was a storage room. A door at the back led to the alley.

"'Don't call the cops or Fido here gets it'?" I looked at Marco. "Maybe you shouldn't watch so much Nick at Nite?"

"Hey, it worked, didn't it?" Marco scratched Champ's neck. "We've got the dog, and your mom's not calling 911. Demorph already. He's not going to stay this calm forever."

I demorphed and flapped onto Champ's back. He was starting to come out of the trance. He whined and tried to pull away from Marco. I sank my talons into his fur. His head drooped again.

I absorbed his DNA, swooped to the floor, and focused on Champ.

My beak stretched into a snout. The tip softened to form a wet, black nose. Forty-two teeth erupted from my jaws.

Schooooooomp! My tail shot out. Long, thin, and naked. The feathers on my head darkened, dissolved, and spiked into dog hair. It covered my body in a wave, down my back, across my wings, to the tip of my curved tail.

I wagged it. I was a dog on both ends — a hawk-sized dog — but still a bird in the middle. A bird covered in coarse black fur.

"Eeeeewwww." Marco. "Nightmare on Sesame Street."

"Yip!" I sounded like a Chihuahua.

My body bulged out and up. The concrete floor receded below me. Internal organs gurgled and crunched, shifted and re-formed. My legs shot up. Wings shot out. Thickened. Realigned. Hollow bones solidified. I thumped down onto four big, steady paws. I was a German shepherd.

With shepherd senses. The eyes were okay. Not as sharp as my hawk eyes. And I couldn't see much color.

But the ears! I could hear coins jingling out at the cash register. A faint breeze whistling across the roof.

And I could smell . . . everything. Mice, yes. Dust. The Dumpster out back. Curdled milk not quite masked by bleach water. You think a broom handle doesn't have a scent? It does. A little

woodsy, a little musty, topped with a delicious bouquet of hand perspiration from every employee who'd ever swept the store.

And Marco's bare feet! Spicy and pungent. And was that — sniff, sniff — had Marco stepped in — sniff — yes! Horse poop! Not recently. Probably several hours ago, at Cassie's barn. But definitely horse.

I was Champ. I had responsibilities. I was steadfast. Noble. I stood at attention while Marco strapped Champ's harness onto my back.

He found a bungee cord and looped it around the real Champ's neck. Champ raised his head and blinked. He was coming out of the stupor.

"How are we going to keep him quiet?" Marco hissed. "He's a smart dog. He'll be on a mission to get back to his master. We can't keep acquiring him over and over."

Ax slid a box from behind his back. "I am truly a juvenile delinquent. I shoplifted these from your mother's basket, Tobias. I apologize."

Dog biscuits!

Champ's tail wagged. He sniffed the box, then sat politely at Ax's feet, waiting for a treat.

I started to salivate myself. <Ax-man, you're brilliant.>

Ax gave Champ a biscuit. Marco held the door open, and I trotted back out into the store.

Back out to my mother.

CHAPTER 22

If you're ever blind, you do not want me as your guide dog. Trust me on this.

I clicked down the grocery aisle toward my mother.

She must've heard me. "Hey, Champ. I knew you wouldn't be gone long." She grasped the handle of my harness. "Forward."

Forward. Okay. This I could do. She was speaking English. I understood English. This wouldn't be too hard. I trotted down the aisle.

Nearly pulled Loren over on her face.

She grabbed a shelf to steady herself.

Okay, not quite right. I wasn't somebody's pet, strolling through the park on a leash. I was a guide dog. Champ. I had to stay at her side.

She held the handle firmly. "Forward."

Okay. Not so fast this time. I stayed by her side. Right by her side. Almost tripped her. She lost her balance and stomped down on my paw. Hard.

"ArrRRRF!" I squealed.

"Oh, Champ! I'm sorry, boy. I didn't mean to smash your poor foot."

She leaned over and reached for me. Took my head between her hands.

And I nearly passed out.

For the first time in my memory, my mother was touching me, and it was just as I'd always imagined it would be.

Okay, so I never imagined I'd be covered in fur, puffing dog breath in her face. And the 7-Eleven wasn't part of the deal, either. In my fantasy, it was always nighttime, and she was tucking me into my race car bed. Yeah, I always wanted one of those red plastic race car beds. Seriously uncool, I know. Shoot me.

But I always imagined her holding my face in her hands, just like she was doing now. And then, in my imagination, she'd pull me close and kiss my nose.

Which is exactly what she did. Loren pulled my face to hers and planted a soft kiss on the tip of my rough, black nose. My dog body trembled. A soft whine bubbled up from my throat.

"Those guys really shook you up, didn't they, boy?" She hugged my neck. "It's okay now. They're gone."

I barely breathed. My mother was reassuring me, loving me.

Yeah, I know. She wasn't really loving me. She was loving her guide dog.

But I was the one standing there. I pushed all thoughts of the real Champ to the back of my mind and just let her pet me. Let her soft voice float through me.

"Feeling better, boy? Let's go home." She stood up and grasped the harness handle. "Forward."

And I stepped forward. Didn't trip her. Didn't run out ahead. I stayed at her side. Led her to the cash register. Led her home.

The bag lady tailed us, of course. We passed the kid at the bus stop. And the broken-down van. But nobody seemed to notice anything new.

We climbed Loren's front steps and entered the house.

Loren's house. I'm not sure what I expected. But what I got was . . . nothing. No pictures on the wall. No mementos or souvenirs. No rugs.

We were in the living room. It could've been any of the places I'd lived with my aunt or uncle. Faded, peeling wallpaper. Stained ceiling. Warped hardwood floor.

The difference was that this room was clean. No newspapers and beer cans strewn over the floor. No laundry baskets spilling underwear onto the couch. No dirty dishes stacked on the tables. Everything was neat. In its place. One square brown couch. One lumpy, worn easy chair. One tidy wooden desk. All placed on one side of the room, leaving a wide, straight path from the front door to the kitchen.

Loren hung her purse on a hook by the door. She unstrapped the harness and hung it up, too. I was glad. I'd been wondering how I was going to wriggle back into that thing every two hours when I had to demorph and remorph.

She carried the grocery bag into the kitchen. I clicked along behind her, sniffing and snooping. Looking for something out of place. Something that proved she was a Controller. Yeah. I seriously wanted evidence that my mother was controlled by a Yeerk.

Because here's the thing. I'd been through this before. I'd been told I had a cousin, a cousin who wanted to adopt me. Raise me. Maybe even . . . love me.

Hah. The loving cousin turned out to be Visser Three, the guy who recently became Visser One. The whole thing was a trap.

So no matter how nice my mother seemed, no matter how good she was at petting her dog, I knew better than to let myself get sucked in by fantasies of a warm, fuzzy family life. A mother who doesn't want you is one thing. A mother who's infested with an evil, parasitic alien is a whole different kind of problem.

But I found nothing. No portable Kandrona. No leftover scent of Hork-Bajir. Nothing to link her to the Yeerks.

She puttered around the house. Put away the groceries. Fixed dinner. I used the bathtub to demorph and remorph. Grasped the shower curtain in my teeth and wrapped it around me while I changed from dog to bird to dog again. Just in case anyone was watching.

When Loren finally went to bed, I demorphed again, but instead of remorphing Champ, I morphed myself. My human self.

I needed hands.

I searched Loren's house thoroughly and methodically, starting at the front door, ending at the back. Closets. Kitchen cabinets. Medicine chest. Refrigerator. Purse.

I told myself I was still looking for signs of Yeerks. And I was. But the truth is, I wanted more than that. I wanted an explanation. An explantion of her life. An explanation of why I wasn't in it.

And at the bottom of a desk drawer, tucked under a row of hanging folders, I found it. A fat brown envelope. I pulled it out. Blew the dust off. Opened it. It was full of medical reports, doctor bills, invoices from a lawyer.

And a letter. Yellowed at the edges. The paper cracked where it had been unfolded and refolded several hundred times. It was from an insurance company, addressed to my mother.

Enclosed please find final payment for injuries suffered in an automobile accident on June 12.

We acknowledge that you have suffered brain damage and loss of vision; however, these conditions are permanent and irreversible. Further medical attention is not authorized. Your claims of total amnesia cannot be proven, and reconstructive surgery is not covered under your group policy.

The enclosed sum terminates our liability in this incident.

I stared at the letter. Amnesia. My mother had amnesia. What did that mean? That she didn't remember anything that happened before the accident? She didn't remember . . . me?

But she must. I was her son. Somewhere inside her damaged brain, she had to have some memory of me. Didn't she? A sliver of memory stored in a healthy brain cell? Somewhere?

She had to. I'd talk to her. Yeah. First thing in the morning. Jake wouldn't like it, but Jake wasn't here. And this was my mother. Maybe my voice or just my presence would bring something back. One tiny memory.

Okay, so I'd been watching too many soaps with Ax. I'd seen too many cases of TV amnesia cured by a visit from a long-lost love. But if it happened on TV, why couldn't it happen for me?

CHAPTER 23

The window shade in the kitchen glowed pink in the morning sun. I morphed my human self again. Made a pot of coffee. Poured myself a cup. Like I needed caffeine. I took a seat at the kitchen table. And waited.

My mother was an early riser. Thank God. I'm not sure how long I could have sat there before I either peed my pants or spontaneously combusted. I heard her bed squeak. Heard her bare feet pad toward the kitchen.

She stopped inside the door and pulled her robe around her. "Who is it?" She didn't sound afraid. Just puzzled. I guess she figured a burglar or a chainsaw murderer wouldn't stop to brew a pot of java.

"It's Tobias." My voice cracked. Oh, yeah, I was really ready for this. "Your son."

She reached for a kitchen chair. Sank into it. "Tobias." Pain washed over her face. "I wondered if you'd ever find me."

I stared at her. "You remember me. You know who —"

"No." She shook her head. "Not the way you think. I know I have a son. I know his name is Tobias. But that's all I know. They brought a little boy to me after the accident. A baby really. They told me he was mine. I didn't remember him. I wanted to. I tried to. But I didn't. I don't remember anything of my life before the accident."

I swallowed. "Even now? I mean, it's been a long time. Didn't any of it ever came back?"

She frowned. Sat silently for a long moment. "There were images. Vague. Half-formed. A tow-headed boy."

My hand rose, almost involuntarily, and touched my blond hair.

She nodded. Like she'd read my mind. "It could have been you. I don't know. It's all so distant. The other images were terrifying. Aliens."

Aliens? I sat very still.

"Sounds crazy," she said. "I know. But that's the only way I could describe them. Which, of course, sent my doctors scrambling for more tests and convinced my sister, or whoever she was, that I was completely nuts. But that's what I had in my head. Aliens. Straight from a nightmare."

Yeah. I'd lived that nightmare.

"Look." She pushed herself from the chair and felt for the counter. "I think I know why you're here. You think I abandoned you. And I guess in a way I did." She pulled a cup from the cabinet and filled it with coffee. "But I couldn't raise a little boy alone. I was blind. Permanently. Facing years of physical therapy. You needed someone who could take care of you. Someone who at least remembered you."

"I needed a mother." My voice echoed through the kitchen. I wanted to catch it and pull it back into my throat. But it was too late. It was already out there. Hanging.

Loren stirred her coffee. Her spoon clanked against the cup. She sat back down at the table.

"When I lost my memory," she said, "I didn't just forget the people I'd known and the things I'd done. I lost things that were much more basic. Like brushing my teeth. Somebody had to teach me how to brush my teeth. But first they had to explain what a tooth was. I had no idea what these little hard things in my mouth were called." She let out a breath. "There's no way I could have raised you."

I nodded. Made sense. In my head. My heart

took a little more convincing. "But you never even, I mean, you didn't —"

"Visit? I know. I was in the hospital for a long time. When I got out, I didn't know where you were. They sent you to stay with my sister, but I didn't know her address. I didn't even know her last name. The hospital didn't have it on file. Maybe I could've tried harder. I just thought — hoped — you were happy. With people who cared about you. Who at least knew who you were. You didn't need a crazy, blind woman in your life."

Yes, I did. Yes. I did.

I still did.

"That stuff doesn't matter anymore," I said. "What matters is that you're in danger. I can't explain it now, and you wouldn't believe me anyway, but I've got to get you out of here."

"Out of here?" She held up her hands. "Whoa. Slow down. What are you talking about?"

"You're not safe here," I said. "I've got to get you out. Soon. I'll figure out how. But right now we have to go for a walk in the park so you can get your real dog back."

"My real dog?" She frowned. "Champ?"

"Yeah. Don't worry. He's safe. The, um, replacement dog will take you to him. Then you have to come back to the house and stay. Don't leave. Don't even go outside. Promise me this. My friends and I will be watching. We'll have to cut your phone line, just to be safe. I won't let anything happen to you, but we have to make sure you're not a Controller."

"A what?" She was either an incredible actress, or she had no idea what I was talking about. "Look, I don't know what you think you're doing, but —"

"Just stay inside," I said. "For two days. Then take another walk in the park."

"Okay, now you're the one who's talking crazy. You say you're my son, and maybe you are. I have no way of knowing. But I'm not going anywhere. This is where I live. This is my life. And you will not cut my phone line."

She was right. It did sound nuts.

I took a deep breath. "Those strange alien images in your head. Huge, right? Leathery. With blades. Like razors, erupting from their skin."

She frowned. "Who told you this?"

"Nobody. Nobody had to. I've seen them. I don't know what the doctors said after the accident, but those images weren't caused by your head injuries or by medication. And you aren't crazy. They're real memories of real aliens."

She sat still. Said nothing.

"You described them as nightmares," I said. "But were there any other images? One that wasn't a nightmare? One that seemed kind? Honorable, maybe?"

She nodded. Slowly. "It's so vague. No form. Nothing recognizable. I've never told anybody about it. It's just a . . . a feeling, almost. A flash."

"A flash of blue?" I said.

She nodded again. She rose from the table and set her cup in the sink. "Two days from now? In the park?"

"Yeah."

She pushed her hair behind her ear. Chewed the edge of her lip. "I'll be there."

CHAPTER 24

<I can get her out.>

Jake looked up at me. Didn't say anything. Yet.

We were in the Hork-Bajir valley. I'd flown there after we'd switched guide dogs. Loren and Champ were back home. Under surveillance by an osprey perched on Ricky Lee's roof and a northern harrier roosting on the garage behind Loren's house.

Jake was sitting in the grass high on the side of the valley, his back propped against a tree. I perched on a branch above him.

<It won't be easy,> I said. <The Yeerks are watching her. But she's not a Controller.>

Jake stripped the head off a dandelion and

tossed it into the grass. "You don't know that, Tobias."

<Yeah,> I said. <I do.>

Why? Because she loved her dog? Because her hands were warm and gentle when she petted him? Petted me?

<I was there for hours,> I said. <Overnight. She never slipped. Never acted like anything but a regular, noninfested sightless person on a limited budget.>

"Doesn't mean anything."

<And I searched her house. No portable Kandrona.>

"She could be storing it someplace else. That church maybe. Or the van across the street."

<Maybe.> I considered that. <But I don't think —> It was hard to admit out loud. <I don't think the Yeerks want her. Not as a Controller. She's blind. To them she's worthless.> I gazed out across the valley. <Besides, she's been under surveillance for over twenty-four hours. Ax and Marco are watching her now. If she doesn't leave her house for another two days, we'll know for sure.>

Jake nodded. "And so will the Yeerks. Even if she's not a Controller, they'll figure it out. They'll be waiting for you. You have to walk away, Tobias. Forget her."

<Like you've forgotten your parents? And Tom?>

He froze.

<You haven't forgotten your family, Jake, no matter what you say. And I can't forget mine. I'm getting her out.>

"How? You said it yourself. She's blind. How can you get a blind person out while the Yeerks are watching?"

<By taking a huge risk. One you probably won't like.> I dug my talons into the branch. <By asking you to trust me.>

He looked up. Met my gaze. Comprehension crossed his face. He knew what I was planning.

"Take Rachel," he said. "You'll need her talons."

I soared out over the valley. Over the free Hork-Bajir who were scurrying around like carpenter ants, helping Marco's dad build cabins for Cassie's and Rachel's families.

It was weird. Another irony. The sudden evacuation of our families had devastated the Animorphs. Put us on edge.

But it had energized the Hork-Bajir. One group was using a meadow at the end of the valley for combat training. They looked like switchblades kick boxing.

Toby, the young Hork-Bajir seer, had organized another group to debrief Marco's mom. Eva had been Visser One's host body for years. She'd seen everything the former Visser One had seen. She knew the Yeerk organization, the Yeerk fleet, and the Yeerks' future plans. And Toby was determined to pick every shred of that information from her brain.

Another group followed Cassie and her family around like a litter of puppies. Large, razor-edged puppies. The Hork-Bajir were crazy in love with Cassie's parents.

Rachel's mom they weren't so smitten with. Still, she had her own group of big, bladed folks. They'd decided her legal expertise was the answer to their self-governing dilemma. They needed a constitution, and they wanted her to draft it. They'd set up an office on the picnic table in the center of camp.

Rachel sat in a lawn chair off to the side. I swooped down and perched on the arm.

"My mom." Rachel waved a hand toward the picnic table. "Thomas Jefferson in heels."

<How are they doing?>

She shrugged. "There's an awful lot of discussion about bark and when you can strip it, and how much, and where. We're a long way from 'We, the People.'"

She leaned her head back against the chair. "Please say you've come to rescue me from this place, Tobias. I've done nothing here but baby-sit

my sisters and listen to my mother grouse about unsanitary bathroom conditions. Tell me you need my help. Tell me you're planning some senseless, suicidal mission. Tell me you can't pull it off without me."

<All of the above,> I said. <For two days. I need your eyes, and I need your talons.>

"Thank you. THANK you." She closed her eyes. "You've saved my sanity."

"Oh, for pete's sake." Rachel's mother tossed down her pen.

An argument had broken out between two groups of Hork-Bajir, the deciduous faction and the coniferous faction. They shouted and shook their clawed fists at each other.

Rachel's mom rubbed her temples.

<I almost feel sorry for her,> I said.

"Don't." Rachel laughed. "She loves this kind of stuff. You're looking at one happy, driven woman. When the bickering stops, that's when she's miserable."

<Ah. Must be genetic.>

CHAPTER 25

We huddled in the semidarkness. In the pedestrian tunnel that ran under the street, connecting one side of the park to the other. I was in guide dog morph. Rachel and Marco were human.

Ax was a northern harrier, perched on Ricky Lee's roof three blocks away, waiting for Loren and Champ to take a walk.

We'd watched her house for two days. She hadn't come out. No one had gone in.

And now we were waiting for her in the park. The same park I used to come to when I lived with my uncle. The same tunnel. Clammy cement. Broken bottles. A sliver of sunlight piercing the

gloom at each end. The perfect place to hide when I needed to escape my life.

Or needed to help my mother escape hers.

And yeah, I was getting really tired of all the irony.

<She has entered the park.> Ax's thought-speak rang through my head. <The female street person is following.>

My ears pricked up. Footsteps. Two sets. A human in sneakers and a quadruped with sharp toenails. Across the sidewalk. Down the steps. The sliver of sunlight disappeared. Two figures entered the tunnel. Loren and Champ.

Loren knew the drill. She'd been here two days earlier, when we returned Champ to her. She made her way to the center of the tunnel and held out the harness handle.

Rachel grabbed it. She and Marco worked like a pit crew at a NASCAR race. Rachel slipped a collar and leash around Champ's neck. Marco unfastened his harness.

<Tobias's mother has been inside the tunnel for twelve seconds,> said Ax. <The female street person is approaching.>

Marco set the harness on my back. Rachel slipped something small and heavy into Loren's bag.

<Eighteen seconds.>

Marco strapped the harness. Rachel slid the handle into Loren's hand.

<Twenty-three seconds. The street person has reached the tunnel. She has stopped at the top of the steps.>

Marco pulled a handful of dog biscuits from his pocket. Rachel placed her hand on Champ's head. The real Champ. He fell into an acquiring trance.

"Go," Rachel hissed.

Loren grasped the handle. "Forward."

I stepped forward and led her to the other end of the tunnel.

<Twenty-nine seconds.>

We emerged into the sunlight.

I glanced across the street. The bag lady had started down the steps. She saw us and froze. She glared at us, scrambled back up the steps, and grabbed her shopping cart.

Loren and I finished our stroll in the park, then headed home. The bag lady followed at a distance. A northern harrier floated through the sky above us.

Loren's street hadn't changed much over the last two days. The teenager's bus still hadn't come. The van was apparently still abandoned. But while we were at the park it had mysteriously moved from the vacant lot across the street to the curb directly in front of Loren's house.

I led Loren inside, just like a good guide dog. As soon as the door clicked shut and she'd unstrapped my harness, I bolted toward the kitchen. No Yeerks. The bedroom. The bathroom. Nothing suspicious.

I returned to the living room.

<The clock's ticking,> I said. <We gotta get out of here.>

"Tobias? Your voice sounds, well, it doesn't sound. It's just sort of there. In my head. And it seems like . . . like you're the dog." She sighed. "I am crazy."

<No, you're not. I'm communicating in thought-speak. Yes, I am the dog. And it's nowhere near as crazy as it's going to get. Put your hand on my face — on the dog's face — and leave it there. Trust me.>

Trust me. I'd been saying that a lot lately. I wasn't even sure I trusted myself.

<The Yeerks are on the move.> Rachel's thought-speak thundered from the roof. <Tick-tock, Tobias. Ticktock.>

Loren stretched one hand out and rested it on my face, palm on my snout, fingers splayed across my forehead.

I focused on red-tailed hawk.

The fur under Loren's fingers liquefied. Dissolved into a black pool and congealed. A feather pattern swept across my body, like a tattoo.

"Ah!" Loren snatched her hand back.

<It's okay, Mo — Moth —> I stumbled over the word. <It's okay, Loren. It feels weird, but it's okay.>

She nodded. Placed her hand on my head again.

<They're onto us!> Marco this time. <Cars screaming in from all directions.>

I pushed his thought-speak out of my head. Focused. My body shrank.

Crrrrunch! My snout slammed back into my skull. Hardened into a sharp, curved beak.

Loren's face twisted in horror. I could feel her trembling. But she didn't remove her hand.

CHAPTER 26

<This is not a test, Tobias. GET OUT!>

I concentrated and finished the morph.

<Okay.> I flapped up onto the couch. <We've got to make this fast. There's a heavy box in your purse. Get it out.>

She nodded, reached into her bag, and pulled out a small blue cube.

The morphing cube. It was one of the reasons I needed Rachel. It was too big and too heavy for a red-tailed hawk. Rachel had carried it from the Hork-Bajir valley in her eagle talons.

<Set it down,> I said, <and place your hand on it.>

Loren set the cube on the couch and pressed her hand flat against the top.

"Ooh!" she started. "It shocked me."

<It does that,> I said. <But it won't hurt you. Leave your hand there.>

<Tobias, you are in danger.> Ax's thought-speak was tense. <You must evacuate.>

Sirens wailed. A few blocks away. Speeding closer.

<Now take your hand off,> I told Loren, <and place it on my head. On the bird's head. I'm standing on the couch.>

She nodded. She looked confused. But she did it.

<Chopper!> said Marco. <Headed our way. Tobias, buddy, you're so out of time.>

<Okay.> I kept my thought-speak even. <Keep your hand pressed against my feathers and concentrate. Think about the hawk. Focus on how the hawk feels under your hand.>

She frowned. "Is this some kind of weird touch therapy?"

<No, it's not therapy. Believe me.>

Loren pressed her hand against my feathers. Her forehead wrinkled in concentration.

THWOK! THWOK! THWOK! Helicopter blades.

<Just think about the hawk,> I told Loren.

<TOBIAS.> Ax was beyond stressed.

<Okay, next step,> I said. <Take your hand from my head, but keep concentrating on the

hawk. Focus. Tightly. Let the hawk surge through you.>

Let the hawk surge through you? No wonder she was skeptical. I sounded like some Psychic Network freak fortune-teller.

But it worked.

Loren's skin darkened to the hawk's dusky brown. An outline of feathers etched itself across her body.

She clutched her arm. Raked her fingers over the feather pattern. "What's happening to me?"

<It's the hawk, Mo — Loren.> Man. What was it with that word? <It's the hawk. You absorbed my DNA, and now you are becoming a red-tailed hawk.>

"I'm WHAT?"

Cars screeched to a stop. Doors slammed. I heard footsteps. Shouts.

THWOK! THWOK! THWOK! THWOK! The helicopter was above the house now.

But inside, I was calm. Determined, yes. Realistic. But not panicked. I was like . . . Jake.

Yeah, Jake. Because now I had the one goal Jake had always had. To save my family.

<Do you hear what's going on outside?> I said.

Loren nodded.

<Those are not nice people. If they catch us,

they will kill us. Or worse. What are you more afraid of? The hawk? Or them?>

Loren took a deep breath. The ridged scars on her face smoothed out. Flattened. Her skull crunched and molded itself into a streamlined hawk head. The feather pattern solidified and burst from her skin.

<Oh, God,> she said. <This is beyond horror.>

<Concentrate,> I said.

Suddenly, her body shrank to the floor. Legs narrowed. The skin covering them hardened into scales. Toes shot out into long talons.

The morph was complete. She was a hawk. A red-tailed hawk.

Exactly like me.

<Tobias?> Her thought-speak was a whisper. <It can't be true.> She blinked her fierce eyes. <I can see. I can see. Tobias, I can see!>

Ka-BOOM.

The entire front wall of the house splintered and crashed to the floor of the living room.

CHAPTER 27

<Excuse me. Coming through. Sorry for the emergency remodeling.>

Rachel! She barreled through the opening in the front of Loren's house. Thundered across the rubble, grabbed the morphing cube in her elephant trunk, and charged out through the kitchen, widening doors along the way.

THWOK! THWOK! THWOK! THWOK!

The downdraft from the helicopter blasted through the house. The street was jammed with police cars and SUVs. Human-Controllers streamed across the yard, Dracon beams pulled. They obviously weren't worried about causing a scene. In this neighborhood, nobody bothered to report anything.

<What do we do?> Loren said worriedly.

<Fly.>

<I don't know how.>

<You don't, but the hawk does. FLY!>

She spread her wings. Flapped. Rose from the hardwood floor. Up. Above the couch.

<I — I'm flying. I can't believe it. I'm really flying!>

<Yeah. Great, isn't it? Now let's get out of here. Stay on my tail. And stay low.>

We flapped toward the kitchen. Skimmed along baseboards. Around the corner. Shot over the tile floor and out the gaping hole Rachel had thoughtfully created for us in the back wall.

Tseeeeeeew!

A Dracon beam blasted overhead. Chunks of Sheetrock pelted our wings.

<My God!> Loren cried. <They're shooting at us!>

<Uh, yeah. They do that sometimes.>

I powered my wings. Loren stayed on my tail. Controllers charged around the corner of the house. Into the backyard.

"There they are! Two hawks."

"GET THEM!"

Tseeeeeeew! Tseeeeeeew!

A clothesline pole exploded.

We shot through the alley. Around a garage. Loren fought the wind. Fought the exhaustion in

her wings from flapping, endlessing flapping. Fought to stay airborne.

<I can't fly this low!>

<Yes, you can. Tip your tail down slightly. Cup your wings. Let the bird mind take over. Let the hawk fly.>

<Hawk. Fly.> Fatigue drained her thought-speak. But she kept pumping. Kept flying.

We shot between two houses. Across a street. Dove behind a line of trees and over a wooden fence. Skimmed along near the ground.

"Where'd they go?"

"Don't know. I lost them."

"Spread out! They couldn't have gotten far."

Feet shuffled through grass and gravel. The fence groaned. Someone was climbing over.

We sailed through the weeds, close to the fence. It ended at a brick wall. A shed. There was an opening at the edge. A board that had rotted and fallen off. I darted through. Loren followed.

We were in an alley. Two patchy strips of gravel, lined with weeds and rusting appliances. Skinny trees formed a spindly canopy over our heads.

We soared past sheds. Garages. Empty lots.

Behind us an SUV crashed into the alley.

"There! Both of them. GO! GO! GO!"

Ahead, open daylight. A street. Cars.

We shot across four lanes of traffic. Into the parking lot of a deserted strip mall on the other side.

We pumped our wings. Jetted around light poles, parking meters, and the burned-out neon mall sign: HILLCREST CENTER, A SHOPPER'S PARADISE.

Tseeeeeew!

Dracon beam fire. The asphalt disintegrated below us.

<The overhang!> I shouted.

The mall was U-shaped, the walkway in front of it covered by a warped metal awning. We dove under it.

<Stay up,> I said. <Where they can't see us.>

We skimmed the storefronts, dodging wires and metal bracing. Turned the corner of the U.

Tseeeeew!

A plate glass window exploded below us.

We reached the end of the building. The end of our cover. Daylight. We shot around the corner. Around the building. Into the service alley behind it.

<NO!> Loren screamed.

I wheeled. Loren raked her talons forward. Raised her wings. Spun around. She was learning fast.

The other end of the alley was barricaded by squad cars. Controller squad cars.

We rocketed back the way we had come.

More Controllers poured in from that end, Dracon beams aimed.

I spun. On one side, a concrete wall. On the other, the back of the shopping center. At both ends, Controllers.

<Sky!> I shouted. <It's the only way.>

I powered my wings. Climbed. Loren beside me.

Up. Up!

And the chopper bore down on us.

CHAPTER 28

The chopper's downdraft pounded us. Loren skidded against the building. I pitched. Rolled. Righted myself.

The pilot leaned from the helicopter. It was the granny-Controller. She raised her Dracon beam.

Tseeeeeeeeeeeew!

The shot seered past my wings. Blasted a crater in the alley. Chunks of asphalt, like shrapnel, pummeled my feathers. I reeled. Loren spun. Granny-Controller aimed again.

<Down!> I shouted.

I dove into the narrow space between a Dumpster and the cinder block wall of the shopping center. Loren plunged in after me.

<What now?>

<Don't know.> My heart pounded in my ears. My wings were numb. <Can't stay here. Let me think.>

Tseeeeeeeeeeeew!

The Dumpster exploded. Hurled us against the wall.

Shouts. Pounding footsteps. A siren. I couldn't tell where the noises were coming from. Wind from the chopper blades whipped through the alley. Peppered us with gravel.

Suddenly: <Tobias! This way!>

<Marco?>

<Back the way you came,> he said. <Behind the old toy store. Loading dock. NOW!>

I lifted my wings. They were heavy with grit. Slowly I rose from the rubble, Loren beside me. Two battered hawks scudded along the pavement toward the abandoned toy store.

"There they are!"

"After them!"

Controllers swarmed toward us from both ends of the alley.

Tseeeew!

The pavement erupted behind us.

"Hold your fire! IDIOTS! You'll shoot each other."

We swooped past a set of metal steps. Up.

Onto the loading dock. Against the heavy steel door. No way through. No way out. Controllers sprinted toward us. Leaped for the dock.

<LOOK OUT!> Loren screamed.

A Controller lunged.

Tseeeeeew!

I dove. Raked my talons across his bald head.

"AAAAAAAAHHHHHH!" He hurtled backward, off the loading dock.

<MARCO! WHERE ARE YOU?>

Sccuuurrrrrruuuunch-BAM!

The steel door behind me ripped. Twisted. Rumbled open.

<IN!>

Loren darted through the door. Didn't question the gorilla standing under it. Or the furry blue alien standing beside him with the Barney backpack strapped to his shoulders.

Fwap! Fwap!

Ax whipped his tail forward. Two Controllers fell from the loading dock, unconscious.

Marco rolled a plastic bin onto the dock. Dumped it over the edge. Hot Wheels cars skittered across the pavement.

Controllers raced over them. Skidded. Teetered. Smack! Hit the ground. Like an old Three Stooges movie.

<GO!>

Marco leaped back into the building. Ax and I followed.

Marco slammed the door down.

We were in a warehouse. Rows of steel shelves towered to the ceiling. Loren was perched on top of the nearest one, waiting.

I jetted past her. <Let's get out of here!>

We swooped over shelves. Around beams. Ax and Marco bounded along below, the backpack bouncing against Ax's shoulders. It looked almost empty, except for something square, and heavy at the bottom. The morphing cube.

<It's about time.> Rachel, still in elephant morph, was waiting at the front of the warehouse. An elephant-sized hole had been ripped through the wall behind her.

<Sorry I couldn't help you back there,> she said. <I couldn't squeeze through all those shelves. Seems I've gained a little weight.>

Tssseeeeewww!

Ka-BOOOOOM.

The loading dock door exploded behind us. Controllers poured into the warehouse.

Rachel lowered her big gray head and pushed against the nearest shelf.

It tipped. Smashed against the next shelf. And the next. The entire row of shelves toppled like dominoes.

"LOOK OUT!" Controllers scrambled back onto the dock.

<LET'S GO!>

We darted through Rachel's hole and into the abandoned store beyond. Ax and Marco raced down one of the aisles. Loren and I flew above, dodging light fixtures and cobwebs. Rachel brought up the rear. Half the shelves were still lined with dust-coated toys. Rachel swung her trunk over them, slinging Legos, golf tees, and Ping-Pong balls onto the floor behind her.

<Uh-oh,> I said. <Trouble.>

Sunlight streamed through the front windows. Outside, four Controllers sprinted toward the store.

CRRRRAAAAAASH.

Heaved a parking meter into the window. Scrambled through the broken glass and charged toward us.

Marco leaped onto a scooter. Grabbed the handle with two huge fingers, held his other fist out, and plowed into the Controllers.

WHAM! WHAM! WHAM! WHAM!

Gorilla fist against human face. All four Controllers dropped to the floor. And they were obviously going to be there for a while.

<You know,> Marco said, <I knew there was a reason I always wanted a scooter.>

THWOK! THWOK! THWOK!

The chopper roared overhead.

Tseeeeeew! Tseeeeeew!

Dracon beams blasted through the warehouse. Controllers stormed us from behind.

Rachel spun around. Took out three Controllers with her massive head.

<Tobias?> Loren wheeled. Flapped above a light fixture. Spun. Flapped back. <TOBIAS!>

<Down!> I said. <Stay DOWN! Don't try to fight these guys.>

She circled. Darted toward an empty bottom shelf.

<Stay there,> I said. <Don't move until I tell you.>

I banked. Two guys lunged at Marco. He slammed one with his fist, the other with his elbow. Another Controller leveled a Dracon beam at his back. I dove.

Tseeeeer!

"Aaaaaaaahhhhh!"

Nailed his trigger finger with my beak. The weapon skidded across the floor.

A floor littered with unconscious Controllers. Ax struck with his tail blade. I raked with my talons. Rachel and Marco beat their attackers back with sheer size and brute strength. Controller after Controller fell. But more kept coming. Pouring in from the warehouse.

<They are trying to force us into the parking lot,> Ax said.

<Yeah.> Thump. Marco's forearm connected with a Controller's gut. <Where the little old chopper pilot can mow us down.>

<So let's give them what they want,> I said. <Out the front. Into the parking lot.>

<ARE YOU INSANE?> Marco, of course.

<Yeah,> I said. <Aren't you?>

CHAPTER 29

<I've got more flight time than any chopper pilot alive,> I said. <Let's see how low she'll go.>

I left Loren in her hiding place. Left Marco, Ax, and Rachel behind to fend off the ground troops.

I shot through the shattered window. Under the awning. Into open daylight. Nothing but sky and pavement.

And helicopter.

A helicopter that would hunt us down no matter where we ran. Out the front. Out the back. It didn't matter. The chopper'd be all over us. We couldn't escape it.

We could only destroy it.

I pumped my wings. Swooped above the metal awning. A handful of Controllers had been posted around the perimeter. They glanced at me, but seemed more worried about the chopper. It spun around. The Controllers dove for cover.

The pilot — our old friend, the granny-Controller — stayed well above the light poles. I saw her lean forward. Glare at me. My hawk eyes could see her grip the control stick in one bony hand. Raise her Dracon beam in the other. Could see her nose hairs twitch as she flared her nostrils in a triumphant sneer.

I swept around the U shape of the mall.

Granny glanced at her instrument panel. Glanced at me.

I spun. Doubled back. I needed her attention. Needed her to focus more on me, less on where the helicopter was flying. Needed her to drop closer to the ground.

She wheeled. Leaned from the door, weapon at the ready. The Controllers hit the pavement.

She aimed. Squeezed the trigger.

Up! I tilted my wings and shot toward the clouds.

Tseeeeeew!

The Dracon beam singed my tail.

Vaporized the front wall of an old diner. Pummeled one of the Controllers with flying debris. The other Controllers bolted for the street. Beyond psycho-Granny's line of fire.

I banked. Dove. Skimmed the asphalt. Shot

under the chopper. The downdraft whipped at my feathers.

The helicopter pitched forward. Perilously close to the top of a light pole. A Dracon beam flashed in the sunlight.

I banked again.

Tseeeeeew!

A speed bump exploded below me.

The helicopter hovered. Its blades sliced the air. Its landing skids swept the top of the light pole again. Granny ignored the instrument panel. Kept her eyes on me.

One more pass. One more pass and I'd have her. I'd get her lower, get her tangled in light poles and wires. The chopper'd be history, and we'd be out of there.

I heard Rachel's trumpeting over the roar of the chopper. I whirled. The ground battle had spilled from the store, out onto the sidewalk. Rachel wrapped her trunk around a Controller and tossed him up onto the awning.

Granny laughed. Whipped the helicopter around. Swooped toward the toy store.

<RACHEL! WATCH OUT!>

I shot toward the chopper.

<TOBIAS, NO! YOU'LL BE KILLED!> Loren's thought-speak. From somewhere. I couldn't see her.

I fought the downdraft. Fought to stay in the

air. Skimmed across the big bubble window in front of the Granny-pilot.

And aimed my thought-speak at her. <What, you need a bigger target? You can't hit a little bird?>

Her face twisted into a maniacal grin. She shouted something, the words swallowed by the drone of the blades. Waved the Dracon beam over her head.

I spiraled. Shot toward the towering HILLCREST sign.

The helicopter rolled. Turned. Jetted after me.

I wheeled back, in a tight spin. Granny stayed with me. Kept the nose of the chopper on me.

I banked. I was in the middle of an open parking lot. Nowhere to hide.

<TOBIAS!>

Sudden movement. Behind me. Another red-tailed hawk! Loren. She hurtled toward me.

Granny aimed.

Loren dove. Hit my wing. Knocked me away.

Tseeeeeeeeeew!

<NO!>

The Dracon beam tore across Loren's back. She plummeted to the ground in a shower of blood and feathers.

I swooped toward her. She lay still. Motionless. Blood poured from the stump of her wing.

<No,> I whispered. <Please, no.>

Her chest quivered. A breath? A heartbeat?

<Demorph!> I ordered. <Focus on your human self and demorph.>

<Can't.> Her thought-speak was weak. Distant.

<You have to.>

<I'll . . . be blind.>

<You'll be alive.>

The helicopter swept toward us.

<Listen to me.> I kept my voice even. <We don't have time for Biology 101. Morphing is based on DNA. It fixes shattered wings. It should fix your damaged eyes, too.>

<Can't . . . take . . . the risk.>

<It's not a risk. You can morph back. You can always morph back. Please. Mom. Demorph!>

She closed her eyes. And then her feathers faded from brown to pale flesh. Beak softened. Skull stretched into a human head.

THWOK! THWOK! THWOK!

<TOBIAS!> Rachel screamed.

Loren's body grew. Expanded. Her wings snapped, sloshed, and shot out into two human arms.

The chopper swung wide. Maneuvered for a clear shot. The tail section spun around.

<She's gonna crash!>

The tail of the helicopter slammed into the HILLCREST sign.

The sign tilted. The tail tore loose from the fuselage and swung crazily by one bracket.

<Look out!> Marco.

Scrunnnnch!

The bracket ripped free.

Ka-BAMMMM. THUNG-UNG-UNG-UNG.

The tail section dropped. The chopper spiraled out of control. Down. Down. Like a missile, spinning toward Earth.

Spinning toward us. Toward me. And my mother.

The ground quaked. Rachel thundered across the parking lot. <TOBIAS! FLY!>

The scales on Loren's legs melted into human flesh. Her talons dissolved into toes.

She blinked. Took a deep breath. "I can see. I can still see!"

The chopper's black underbelly plummeted toward us.

<Great, but can you run?>

<No time to find out.> Rachel wrapped her trunk around Loren, snatched her from the pavement, and charged toward the other end of the parking lot.

I powered my wings and soared after her.

And the helicopter slammed into the lot. Into the pool of hawk blood where my mother had lain.

And exploded into flames.

CHAPTER 30

"Champ! Here you go, boy. Catch." Loren tossed the Frisbee. It sailed out over a meadow at the edge of camp.

Champ raced after it, leaped, and caught it in his teeth.

We were in the Hork-Bajir valley. Home. We'd been here since the battle at the strip mall.

Getting away was pretty easy once the chopper exploded. The Controllers deserted when they saw it going down. Psycho-granny bailed just before impact. I saw her crawling on her belly across the parking lot. It was a satisfying sight.

We retrieved Champ on the way back. Rachel

had locked him inside an old car that was up on blocks behind somebody's house. He was one happy pup when we let him out. He about wagged himself in half. About licked Loren's face off. He was definitely glad to see her.

And she was glad to see him. Glad? Make that elated, euphoric, ecstatic. She fell to her knees, held his face in her hands, and just looked at him. Looked at him and looked at him and looked at him. Tears rolled down her cheeks. She wrapped her arms around his neck and buried her face in his fur.

And yeah, I admit it. I was jealous. Jealous of a dog. How's that for pathetic?

Now we were back in the valley. Champ bounded through camp, the Frisbee clenched in his teeth. He jostled through a group of Hork-Bajir who'd formed a circle. Rachel's mom stood on a bench in the center.

"No," she was telling them. "No, no, no. Elemenopee is not one letter. L. M. N. O. P. Get it?"

She shook her head and rubbed her temples.

A couple of days ago she'd gotten the kinks worked out of the Hork-Bajir constitution. She'd read it to them. They'd voted unanimously to accept it. She set it on the table, ready to be signed.

And they'd just stood there, confused. Toby,

the seer, was the only Hork-Bajir in the valley who could read or write. The rest of them didn't even know how to hold a pen.

So they voted to have Rachel's mom teach them.

"Excuse me?" Her voice had thundered through the valley. "Do I look like a teacher?"

They voted again, and decided that, yes, she did indeed look like a teacher.

Now she was teaching them the ABC song.

Jake and I sat at the picnic table and watched. I was in human morph. For no reason other than somehow it felt . . . right. I'd never really been comfortable in my human body, even back when I was a regular non-*nothlit* kid. But now, with Loren here, I wanted to at least try it out. For two hours at a time, anyway.

Loren. My mother. I watched her race after Champ. Pull the Frisbee from his mouth and send it sailing across the valley again.

Her scars were gone. Her long blond hair fell shiny and straight down both sides of her head. And she could see. Morphing had restored her vision.

I'd thought — hoped — that it would also restore her memory. But it didn't. She still didn't know me. Didn't remember anything from before the accident.

Cassie had tried to explain it. "Morphing can

fix injuries," she said, "because all the information needed to re-create the cell is stored within your DNA. But memories? How are those stored? As electrical impulses? As part of your soul? When they're gone, maybe they're just . . . gone."

Yeah. Maybe they were. Maybe the little tow-headed kid would never be anything more than an unrecognizable image from a life my mother would never remember.

But she'd thrown her body between me and a Dracon beam. Like Cassie's mom when she saw Ax. Like Rachel's mom with the spice rack. Whether she remembered me or not, loved me or not, my mother almost died trying to save me.

That had to count for something. Didn't it?

"Have you told her about Elfangor?" Jake asked.

"No." I shrugged. "I will. I just haven't figured out how. I mean, how do you tell somebody that she used to be married to an alien? That she loved him and he loved her, and that because of their love, they had . . . me? And then, after getting her all worked up over a husband she can't remember, say, 'Oh! And did I mention he's dead?'"

Jake nodded. He stared out over the camp, at the cabin he shared with Marco and his family.

It was weird. We'd almost traded places. To-

bias the orphan suddenly had a mother. Jake, the poster boy for the all-American nuclear family, was alone. Living in somebody else's house, the way I'd always had to live with one ragtag relative or another. Not knowing where his real family was.

"They're still alive," I said. "We can still save them."

"Can we?" He picked at the splintered edge of the picnic table. "What do you think's going to happen to Tom now that Visser One knows he's been living with an Andalite bandit all this time? How much do you think his life is worth?"

"A lot. That's just it, Jake. Visser One needs him. Needs your parents. Now more than ever. He needs them so he can find us. He needs them to draw us out. As long as we keep fighting, Visser One will keep them alive."

Don't miss

ANIMORPHS®

#50 The Ultimate

"Can you talk to Rachel?" I said quietly to Jake. "She explodes at her mom and it just makes Naomi more determined not to deal with this."

Jake's voice was impatient. "I've tried to talk to Rachel and she won't listen. So, no, I won't talk to her again. And no, I don't want to talk to you about my feelings."

I stood perfectly still, not trusting myself to move. I felt as if I'd been slapped.

Jake lowered his eyes, turned and walked away.

I stalked after him. "Jake! Things are falling apart."

He whirled on me. His eyes were dark and wild. For the first time since I'd known and loved Jake, I was afraid of him. Afraid of what he might become.

"You think I don't know that?! I know we're slipping up. Making mistakes. I know we're at each other's throats. And I know that if it weren't for Toby, this whole camp would probably be just a scar on the ground by now. What I don't know, Cassie, and this is the hard part . . . what I don't know is what I'm supposed to do about it."

I'd heard the expression, "my heart almost broke" . . . Now, I knew what it meant.

I put my anger aside and fell into step beside Jake.

"It's going to take time," I said calmly. "These people, our parents, have been dragged into this war — into a refugee camp — against their wills. Their world has been torn apart. We have to respect their reluctance to fight alongside us. But, Jake, somebody's got to take charge."

"Fine. You do it."

"No," I said firmly. "I'm not a leader, Jake. You are. You're going to have to talk to my parents. And to Rachel's mother and sisters. Even Tobias's mom."

"Why should they listen to me?" Jake countered. "Look at the situation. We're hiding in the forest, living on the charity of the Hork-Bajir. If you were an adult — or even another kid, not Cassie — would you listen to me? No, you wouldn't. So why don't you just leave me alone?"

He looked at me. Then turned his head.

"Please, Cassie."

Jake quickened his step and left me behind.

"Stop feeling sorry for yourself," I called after him. Desperate.

He didn't stop.

"You're acting like a coward!"

The moment the words were out of my mouth, I regretted them.

Jake stopped. Turned. His face was a stranger's. "*What* did you call me?"

He'd heard me. Too late to take back the words. "A coward," I repeated, flinching. "Now that it's the final crisis, you're turning chicken on us."

I didn't expect his weary laugh. "I'm not chicken," he said. "I'm just trying to give everybody a fighting chance. I'm not going to insist people do what I say when I don't have the slightest idea what's right or wrong. What's smart or stupid. Cassie, it's my fault we're on the run. You can't deny that."

I walked up to Jake, took a deep breath, and tried to sound reasonable. Reached for his hand and held it tight.

"Maybe you're right, Jake. And maybe you're wrong. Maybe you are a good leader, after all."

He tried to pull away but I wouldn't let him go.

"No, Jake. Listen. If that's the truth, you have to take charge. And if you really are a failure and it really is all your fault, then it's your responsibility to get us out of here. We need you, Jake. Either way, it has to be you."

It was a cheap shot. Jake's Achilles' heel has always been his sense of responsibility. I could see him weakening.

"Marco can be in charge," he said helplessly. Again he pulled his hand away. This time I let him go. "He's smarter than I am. Or Tobias. Or Ax. Or you. Rachel. Anyone. Anyone but me. You know why I was even in charge in the first place, Cassie? Because once upon a time, a long time ago, Marco said I was."

"Jake, that's not the whole truth . . ."

"Well, now my term of office is over," he continued bitterly. "So how about for once you guys figure things out and tell me what to do."

Then he turned and walked away.

And just kept walking.